Never

Say Goodbye

SARAH GRACE GRZY

Never Say Goodbye

A novel by Sarah Grace Grzybowski

Paperback ISBN: 978-1-0878-7305-3

Cover by Estetico Designs www.esteticodesigns.com
Interior Formatting by Victoria Lynn Designs
www.victorialynndesigns.com
Copy Edit by Bridget Marshall

Printed in the USA

Dedication:

To Isabella Hope. My little sister and bestest friend. Thank you for believing in me when I can't believe in myself. I love you.

Chapter One

Tyler Collens slapped down the sandwich he'd just picked up from the dashboard as the radio crackled on from the center console of the ambulance.

"Dude. I was hoping for a peaceful lunch hour," he groaned. His paramedic partner Ezra Bryant chuckled and picked up the radio. The small town of Arlington, Washington didn't see too many emergencies on any given day, but today they'd been running since the beginning of their shift, and it was only noon.

"Unit three, we have a residential structure fire at one-oh-four South Olympic Avenue. Fire is en route. Reports of smoke in the east end of the complex—"

The dispatcher continued, but the effect of the words sucker punched Tyler in the gut, and he was frozen by the impact. He met his partner's eyes, and

Ezra gave a grim, understanding nod as he signaled the unit's response to the dispatcher, hit the lights and siren, and shifted the vehicle into gear.

"Take a breath, Ty."

Tyler struggled to pull air into his lungs. Panic-induced adrenaline rushed through his body, leaving him feeling unsettled and unsteady. He fought to regain his equilibrium as Ezra navigated to the apartment complex they were both more than familiar with. The dispatcher updated their information when fire arrived on site, and he was minutely relieved to know there were no visible flames.

But smoke inhalation could be more deadly than fire itself.

He dragged in another breath and exhaled. "Murrae." As if he had to say anything.

"I know, man. I know."

Ty white-knuckled the dashboard as Ezra took a turn too quickly. The three-minute ride to the complex felt like an eternity to him. Terrifying thoughts raged through his brain.

I can't do this again, was the foremost one chanting in circles within his cerebrum even as he fought to rein in the panic and let logic take over. Everything was probably fine.

But the thing was, he didn't know.

He was peripherally aware of Ezra's sidelong glances at him during the brief-but-too-long drive. Ezra wasn't just his paramedic partner; he was his closest friend.

They arrived, and Ezra had barely put the rig into park before Ty was out and running toward the fire lieutenant in charge of the scene. He took a quick visual sweep of the area. The situation appeared to be largely under control. Bystanders and residents gathered in groups a safe distance from the building, and many of the firefighters were either packing up their gear or standing around. The lieutenant, a tall man with a commanding aura whom he recognized as Davis Jamentz, stood with his hands on his hips as his gravelly voice barked an order to his men. He turned and caught sight of Tyler, giving him a nod of recognition.

"Collens. Looks like we won't be needing you. The fire was contained to one empty apartment, although there was some minor smoke damage to the surrounding apartments. No one was injured. Your apartment might need some work, though."

"And Murrae?"

The man's face morphed into some combination of compassion and contrition. "Oh, sorry, man. She's fine. She's with her caretaker." He pointed in the direction of the crowd.

Tyler blew out a breath. The adrenaline fading from his body made him feel suddenly tired and so much older than his thirty years. "Thank God," he mumbled.

The lieutenant's nod gestured behind Tyler. "You're released. I'll follow up with your partner."

With relief, Tyler took a step back only to bump into Ezra, who grunted in surprise as he steadied himself. The man was by no means small or puny, but

Tyler's six-four linebacker's frame had a good six inches on him. "Sorry."

Ezra just slapped his shoulder and pushed him in the direction he'd been heading before turning to speak with the lieutenant.

Tyler smiled to himself. Ezra was a good man and a good friend. He jogged in the direction Jamentz had indicated and quickly spotted Ellen Chance, the fifty-some-year-old woman he paid to take care of his daughter while he worked. She caught sight of him and waved.

"Oh, Tyler! I tried calling you but couldn't get through!"

Ty patted his hip where his phone usually resided in a holster. Empty. "I'm so sorry. It must have fallen out again," he said with remorse. He had to stop continually losing the darn thing.

She waved a hand dismissively. "It's all right. I just knew you would be worried when you heard the radio, so I wanted to let you know that we were all right." Tyler shifted the pink blanket on the bundle the woman held in her arms, something in him needing to see the truth before his heart could accept it. "She slept right through the whole ordeal, smoke alarms and all, the dear." Ellen chuckled. She shifted the bundle into Tyler's arms.

The eighteen-month-old stirred enough to sigh sleepily and wrap a tiny arm around her daddy's neck, but didn't wake. Tyler's heart melted as the little girl relaxed into his chest, as if she knew she was right where she belonged. He buried his face into her dark, wispy curls and mumbled a thank you to Ellen. She smiled gently and tucked the blanket a little more securely around the toddler before turning to talk with another resident.

Tyler inhaled deeply, trying to calm the jitters in his hands. He knew from experience that he could handle any emergency situation with the calmness and precision of a professional, but he was disturbed by how this scenario had rattled him.

He'd overreacted.

He walked a few paces away from the crowd, holding his daughter a little closer as a chilly spring breeze blew around them. His heart rate slowed as peace swept through him. Murrae's arms involuntarily tightened around his neck in her sleep as Tyler inhaled the scent of baby shampoo and something fruity. She was all right. So he was all right, and, despite the mess his apartment likely was, his heart was already home.

Several minutes later, Ezra walked up. He tilted his head to look at the sleeping Murrae, and a smile softened his face. "She good?"

Tyler nodded. "Slept through the whole thing, apparently. Ellen got her out before the smoke, so she'll be fine."

Ezra laughed ruefully. "I wish Haevyn slept that well," he said, referring to his three-month-old daughter.

Now that he noticed it, his friend had the dark circles ringing tired eyes that spoke of a parent with a baby. Sympathy twinged as Tyler remembered those sleepless nights he'd had to go through alone.

Ezra shifted and rested a hand on his belt. "Your apartment is not going to be livable for the next while."

Tyler groaned and scowled. "Awesome."

"Yeah. The apartment complex will be responsible for handling everything, but it could be a few days."

"I guess I'll find a hotel or something."

"Or you could stay with us," Ezra offered.

Tyler immediately shook his head. "I wouldn't do that to you guys. Four in that tiny house is already pushing it."

His friend grinned, shrugged, and shoved his hands into his pockets. "Well, I certainly won't make you."

Tyler rolled his eyes. After four years of marriage and two children, the man still acted like a newlywed.

"My dad has room in his townhouse," Ezra said. "You know he's pretty much convinced Murrae is his granddaughter too."

Tyler shook his head again. "I don't want to put him out. I'll just get a hotel for a few nights. Insurance will probably pay for that too, at least partially."

Ezra nodded. "Well, I need to get going. I called the chief and he cleared Jason to fill in for the rest of your shift, so I'll see you tomorrow morning, partner."

Tyler had the sudden urge to cry in gratitude. Wow, that adrenaline rush must have messed with his emotions. He didn't just break down and cry, like, ever. That would be awkward.

"Thanks, Ezra. I owe you one."

Ezra smirked. "No prob. You know I'll collect. Take care." He thumped Tyler on the shoulder—the one Murrae wasn't cuddled up on—and walked away.

Later that night, Tyler laid Murrae in the portable crib the hotel provided. Pacifier in her mouth and her favorite soft blanket clutched in her hands, she blinked up at him sleepily with round blue eyes—pretty much the only physical feature she'd inherited from him. The rest was her mother—everything from her dark hair to her petite features. His heart ached with a pain that was almost physical as he thought back on the scare of the day. She still looked so vulnerable, though her small size was a result of her premature birth. He couldn't imagine his life without this precious soul, but then again, he had thought that about his wife once, and yet here he was.

He ran his finger tenderly down her face one more time before pressing a kiss to her silky-soft skin and flopping onto the bed, having already showered and changed into cotton shorts and a t-shirt. He tugged his phone off the nightstand and opened Spotify. Pressing the green button on his favorite playlist, he tucked the earbuds in his ears. Turning the music up to silence other sounds, he set the phone on the bed next to him and closed his eyes.

A plea he had no words for rose from his heart to the heavens as he drifted off.

Chapter Two

A lyvia Emmerson adjusted the frame she had just hung on the wall behind the front desk of Happy Haven Books. She tilted her head to the right and stared at the piece of hand-lettered artwork featuring a *Pride and Prejudice* quote, smiling in satisfaction now that it was finally hanging straight.

Just two weeks ago, she'd signed the final paperwork that made the small, brick-facade bookstore on E. 5th Street hers and hers alone. The culmination of years of dreams, saving, and hard work. And she was pretty darn proud.

Turning and dusting her hands together—for the satisfaction of the action alone; she had already dusted the place top to bottom—she faced the front counter and adjusted the items on it for the fifth time. She loved being able to spread out and make the store her own with adorable little decorative knick-knacks that her brothers mocked.

But now, two weeks later, some of the euphoria was wearing off as reality set back in with invoices, a leaky roof, a mildewy bathroom, and a broken shelf in the self-help section. Not to mention the upstairs apartment she was getting ready to move into . . . Well, it was from the '70s, to say the least. The good, solid coat of paint it needed was one of the easiest things to knock off her to-do list. She was starting to feel a little overwhelmed.

Okay, a lot overwhelmed.

Giving the bookstore one last survey—empty of customers at the moment—she headed toward the back room where boxes of new books sat on a cart, waiting to be rehomed on shelves. She picked up one heavy box after another and put them on the table. Looking on the bright side, she was getting a decent arm workout on delivery days.

Even as she snorted at the thought, her fingers slipped from the bottom of the third box. The heavy-duty cardboard shipping carton fell to the floor with a hefty thud. The lid slipped off, and books spilled out and slid across the concrete floor.

Alyvia gave a startled gasp that sounded way more dramatic than the moment called for—a trait she had inherited from her dad—and stared. "Oh snap." She gave a frustrated groan. Dropping to her knees, she hurried to carefully restack the scattered books, straightening dust jackets and bent covers. Damaged books were so sad looking, but thankfully there were only a few. She would have to place them in the discounted section.

By the time Alyvia finished unboxing the books, the bell above the door jingled, signaling a customer.

She pushed to her feet, brushed off the knees of her skinny jeans, and hurried to the front. She caught sight of a person disappearing beyond the far wall of shelves and instantly recognized the stooped shoulders and drab yellow knitted sweater.

"Good afternoon, Mrs. Cramer!" she called in the cheeriest voice she could muster, wincing slightly as it came out sounding higher-pitched than she expected. Her drooping mood had suddenly lightened at the thought of the cantankerous older woman.

Mrs. Eliza Cramer was a regular at Happy Haven, and likely their biggest customer, as Alyvia knew from her time working in the store before she had bought it. The woman's voracious reading habit rivaled even her own. But the grouchiness was not something they had in common. Alyvia had made it her personal goal to at least coax a few words from the woman, if not a simple smile.

There was no response to her greeting—as she expected—so she started tidying up the storage shelves underneath the front counter area while she waited. Fifteen minutes ticked by before Alyvia looked up at the sound of shuffling feet. She set aside the book she'd been reading, having burned out on organizational efforts.

"Hi, Mrs. Cramer! Did you find everything you wanted okay?" she asked as the older woman set a stack of six books on the counter.

Mrs. Cramer muttered something vague under her breath that Alyvia wasn't able to catch as she rang up the books.

Alyvia made another attempt in a bright tone. "Have you read anything really good lately?" The pause got awkward, so Alyvia continued. "Well, I just finished Charles Martin's *Send Down the Rain*, and it was *so* good! Have you read it yet? I think you'd probably like it." Being able to recommend her favorite books to her patrons was one of the biggest perks of the job.

The conversation lacklusterly continued, carried almost solely by Alyvia as she bagged the woman's purchases. The bell rang again as Mrs. Cramer left without a backward glance. Alyvia slumped back in her chair.

It was exhausting carrying a conversation by oneself.

She blew out a sigh, then checked the time. Only a few more hours until closing time. Alyvia stood up, stretched, and tried to decide what to tackle next. She hadn't been prepared for the amount of mental and physical energy necessary to fix up and run a bookstore, and she felt a little out of her league. Like, way out of her league, actually. She needed help.

But all of that was a worry for another day. Tonight was going to be her first night staying in the upstairs apartment. She just had a few more things to grab from her mom's house, and then she would be on her own.

For the next two hours, she helped the trickle of Friday night customers, restocked shelves, and continued the process of orienting herself with the computer systems. She would have said she knew her way around computers fairly well, but getting the online system figured out was taking a fair amount of Google troubleshooting.

By the time she finished, it was minutes to closing time, and she hurriedly loaded her essentials into her blue canvas backpack-purse and locked up. She was ridiculously excited at the prospect of grabbing a few things from home, unpacking a bit and settling in, and then making a soothing cup of decaf and putting this busy day to bed—literally—by enjoying one of the new releases she'd just unpacked.

Her car chirped as she pressed the unlock button on the fob, and she dropped her backpack onto the passenger seat before walking around to the driver's side. She checked behind and in front of her before pulling out of her parallel-parking spot and onto one of the main streets through the quaint town of Arlington. It was springtime, but dusk was already starting to settle like smog over the town.

Alyvia flicked on her headlights and merged onto the divided highway leading out of town to her mom's house, empty tonight. Her mom had made the drive into Seattle to see her oldest daughter Maddison's new baby. She wished she had gone to Maddison and Luke's townhouse in Seattle as well. Or that Maddison was here to help her move in and have a girls' night, just like old times. That hadn't happened in too long.

She felt lonely—a strange and uncomfortable feeling that she hadn't experienced much.

Alyvia glanced down at the dash for a brief second to turn the radio on, hoping for something peppy to distract her from her nostalgia. As she looked up, her heart leapt into her throat at the sudden appearance of the brake lights of a car in front of her on the busy divided highway. She slammed on her brakes, but it was too late.

Metal crunched against metal as the cars met in a jolt that rattled her teeth. Her head whiplashed against the back of the seat and the airbag deployed, twisting her arm. A yelp escaped her at the pain.

In the sudden quiet, her harsh breathing sounded like a roar in her ears. She sat there for what felt like an eternity, having to remind herself simply how to breathe. What had even happened? Had she caused the accident? What about the other person? She had only looked down for a moment . . .

Finally, just as sirens started to wail, the adrenaline faded, and a sharp pain raced down her spine. But the achy, throbbing pain in her arm made her breath catch and brought tears to her eyes as she clutched it against her chest.

The blue and red lights of emergency vehicles swirled in the gathering darkness. Having never been in a car accident before, she wasn't sure what to do next. Get out? Sit still? Swallowing against the nausea rising in her throat—from the pain or the fear—she sat still for a moment longer. Closing her eyes, she drew in deep breaths. *Jesus, help. What just happened?*

The driver's side door of the car tugged open, and a familiar voice soothed her. "Alyvia, it's Ezra. Just don't move, okay? Do you have pain anywhere specific?"

Relief washed over her. That was a quick answer to her plea. "Ezra." Tears still ran down her cheeks, but she wasn't even embarrassed by her best friend's husband seeing them. "I'm okay. My arm just hurts a little bit. I twisted it somehow, I think."

"Okay, I'm going to—" He broke off as she started to turn in the seat and found her legs pinned underneath the dash. Panic rose again. "Hey, hey, hey, I said hold still, all right? We'll get you out, but I don't want you injuring yourself any further. Do you have any pain in your neck or back? Your head?"

Alyvia took a deep, shuddering breath, assessed herself, then shook her head. "No. Not really."

"Okay." She caught his nod and saw an officer standing behind him, ready to help. "I'm gonna move your seat back and we'll get you on the gurney."

"No!" She shook her head vigorously, dreading a night in the ER more than anything else at the moment. "I don't want to go to the hospital. I don't need to. I'm fine." She paused, then looked up at him. "You can't make me, right?"

Ezra pursed his lips. "No, I can't make you. But I'd consider it a personal favor if you went and got checked out. This was a bit more than a fender bender. You know Piper'd have my head if I let you go and you weren't actually okay."

His entreating look and the mention of her friend brought a faint smile to her face, and she palmed away the tears drying on her cheeks with her good hand. "Can't you just check me out here and then I can go home?"

"Can do." Ezra gave a mock salute. "We'll get you fixed up and on your way." He glanced away for a moment and waved at someone, then looked back at her. "I've got to go deal with something, but my partner or I will be back in a sec, so just don't go anywhere, 'kay? You know good ol' Ty, right?"

Alyvia nodded. She knew of him by name, mostly. But she was suddenly too tired to explain anything. She squeezed her eyes shut for a brief moment, then opened them when gravel crunched. A ridiculously tall, blond-haired man squatted down at her eye level.

He gave her a friendly grin, but it didn't quite reach his lake-blue eyes. A seriousness . . . a tiredness lurked behind them, as if he felt weary.

"Hey, Alyvia. I'm Tyler. I'll do my best to get you out of here ASAP. Having a bit of a rough day, huh?" He helped her push the seat back and turn so she was sitting sideways, facing him. He shined a penlight into her eyes, and they watered.

"You look like you've had a rough day, too." Oops. She hadn't meant to share her observation. The tiredness in her bones and the ache in her body had removed her filter.

The paramedic pulled back in surprise and looked at her for a moment, then seemed to recover with a shrug and a chuckle. "That was pretty intuitive. I guess we can rule out a concussion." He winked at her as he tightened a blood pressure cuff around her arm.

"Ezra said your arm got twisted a little?" he asked, pointing to where she unconsciously had clutched her left arm protectively against her body.

She noticed how he diverted the conversation. "Yes. My wrist aches a bit, but it's already not as bad as it was."

"Can I look at it?"

She silently shifted the throbbing appendage toward him. He cupped her elbow in one big hand and, with the other, he started gently massaging the muscles of her forearm, testing the bone. His finger found a tender spot, and she hissed in a breath between her teeth. Tyler glanced up at her.

"One to ten, how bad?" he asked.

She thought for a second. "Three?"

His brows raised and his fingers shifted toward her wrist, amusement causing one side of his mouth to edge upward. "Scout's honor?" He started slowly rotating her wrist and she couldn't hold back a wince—although she tried.

"Five? But I was never a girl scout and I think the pain scale is lame."

He chuckled and set her arm back on her lap. "Fair enough. And you're not wrong; it's an imperfect system. Tell you what, I'll wrap that wrist with an elastic bandage, and you promise to head over to an urgent care center or call 911 if your pain increases. If there is any numbness or tingling in your hand, or you begin to feel any other unusual symptoms, you should get it checked out. All right?"

She nodded her agreement. He grabbed an elastic bandage and began firmly wrapping her wrist as he gave her further instructions on caring for the injury.

"I just have a bit of paperwork I need you to sign, but otherwise, you should be good to go." Tyler handed her a clipboard and pen and gave her a smile. Ezra walked up behind him as she skimmed the information attached to the clipboard and scrawled her name and date in three places.

"How's our girl, Ty?"

"I'm fine." Alyvia answered before he could as she handed the clipboard back to Tyler. She looked up at Ezra. "Is the other driver okay?"

"Yeah, they're fine. We're not even going to transport."

She nodded, relief loosening her muscles.

"Do you have someone to come pick you up, Lyv? This old boy doesn't look like it's gonna be road-worthy without a bit of work." Ezra patted the roof of the gray Accord as he leaned in over the opened door to see her better.

Alyvia frowned and paused, considering options that were painfully few. "I . . . don't know. Mom's in Seattle tonight, of course. Aaron's on call this weekend . . ." She thought out loud, feeling stressed, tired, and a headache coming on. She *didn't* want to cry again.

Ezra shifted, propping one hand on his hip. "Well, Ty and I are headed back to the department to end our shift right after we're done here, so one of us could take you home. If you're okay with that. Otherwise I could call Piper, but she's got the kids."

Alyvia's head popped up. "Really? You'd do that? Are you sure?"

"Of course. After you give your statement, Calvin can drop you off at the department, and one of us will take you home. All right?"

"You're the best, Ez." She stood, and the ground rushed up to meet her in the mother of all head rushes. Both men jumped at the same time and each instinctively grabbed an elbow to keep her from falling. When the dizziness faded within seconds, she let out a breathy chuckle. "Whoa."

"You sure you're okay, Alyvia?" Tyler asked. "It's not too late to take you to the ER just to get checked out. It can't hurt."

"No. I'm fine, really, I am. I just stood up too fast. The adrenaline is wearing off."

Tyler looked at Ezra as if for confirmation. Alyvia huffed a breath that was half laugh, half exasperation. "Listen, I'm a grown woman. I can make my own decisions."

Tyler shrugged and Ezra nodded. "Okay. I'll let Calvin know if you're ready to go. Hey, Calvin!" Ezra walked toward one of the squad cars still idling nearby.

Alyvia leaned into her car and grabbed her backpack from the floor where it had fallen. Pausing, she patted the roof of the small car. "Poor Watson," she mumbled. Turning away, she nearly bumped into Tyler, who still stood behind her, one hand holding the red medic bag, the other holding a small ice pack which he snapped over his thigh before handing to her. She took it with a grateful smile. "Thank you, Tyler. Not just for the ice pack."

His eyes crinkled with a small smile. "Not a problem, ma'am." He tipped an imaginary cap toward her, and Alyvia smiled as she headed after Ezra.

What a nice guy.

SARAH GRACE GRZY

Chapter Three

It was quiet except for the peaceful rumble of Tyler's truck. Alyvia had been staring out the window silently for the past few miles, after thanking him more than three times for taking her home.

Tyler still didn't know how he'd been roped into it. His plan was to grab some dinner to go, and spend the rest of the evening peacefully in the hotel room with Murrae.

Honestly though, he was ridiculously excited to be out of that hotel room.

Tyler glanced over at Alyvia. She was probably a couple of years younger than him, but looked even younger. Dark brown hair contrasted with her light olive skin tone, giving her a more distinctive appearance. Her chocolate eyes seemed to have a twinkle in them, adding to the youthful look and giving the impression that she was always cheerful. Her hair had been pulled up into a braided bun of some kind that complimented her round face and she didn't seem to be wearing much makeup. He kind of liked that.

Pushing his eyes back to the road, he cleared his throat, finding the silence awkward. "So. You named your car?"

Alyvia turned in her seat to face him, and he didn't miss the wince she tried to hide. She was likely quite sore from the accident. "Yeah?" Her tone was slightly defensive . . . as if she got teased about the subject often.

He shrugged and offered a conciliatory tone. "I was just . . . curious."

She sighed. "I'm sorry. I'm being grouchy. I've just had . . . one of those days."

Tyler chuckled, understanding. "Eh, I've had my days too."

Alyvia returned to looking out the window for a few silent minutes before turning back again. "Thank you again for—"

Tyler held up a hand and broke off her sentence. "Please. Don't thank me again, or I just might *not* take you home."

She stared at him for a moment, surprised, then laughed. A pleasant sound. "Okay, I won't . . . How many times *did* I thank you?"

"I lost count." They both laughed, and it felt good. Stress had been a far too prevalent emotion in his life for the last couple of months . . . make that years. It felt good to not be stressed, if only for a moment.

They chatted for a few minutes more about trivial things such as the weather—so cliché, Tyler thought—until he pulled into the driveway Alyvia pointed out as her mom's. She gathered her purse and pushed open the passenger side door before turning to him once more. "Tyl—never mind, I won't thank you, as I'm not sure what you'd do. Have a nice evening."

"You, too, Alyvia. It was nice to officially meet you." As she climbed out of the car, he rested his wrist against the steering wheel and added, "You might want to take some ibuprofen or you won't sleep with that soreness."

In the dim evening light, she lifted a brow. "Wow. You're nearly as observant as Ezra."

He laughed. "Only nearly?"

"I swear that man can sense pain. And I'm usually pretty good at hiding it."

"Huh. I'll remember that. You definitely need that ibuprofen then."

She huffed a laugh. "Goodnight, Mr. Collens."

"Goodnight, Miss Emmerson."

The door closed and Tyler let the truck idle as she walked up the sidewalk and unlocked the front door. She glanced back and waved before entering the house. Ty put the vehicle in gear and backed out of the driveway with a sigh.

Now he could go home.

Or rather, to the hotel.

He'd grab something to eat. Take off his paramedic hat and put on his daddy hat. Spend some time with Murrae before her bedtime.

And then he'd put on his lonely hat, sit on the empty, too-soft hotel bed and hope that sleep claimed him before his thoughts did.

He met Ellen with Murrae in the lobby, then took the elevator to their room, his baby girl in his arms. Her lighthearted, unintelligible jabbering lightened his mood considerably.

"Who's Daddy's happy girl?" He nuzzled her neck with kisses. She giggled and pushed away, then patted his cheek.

"Dada." She poked a finger at his stubbled chin. "Dada. Ow."

He chuckled. "You're so smart. Yes, Dada needs to find a razor." Tyler sat her on one of the beds with a toy and quickly changed out of his uniform into jeans and a white t-shirt. He then opened the pizza box he'd picked up on the way in. He cut up a small piece into tiny bites, then put two pieces for himself on a paper plate, joining in with her nonsensical chatter as he did so. He settled with Murrae on his lap at the tiny desk and she excitedly started shoving bites into her mouth.

After dinner and romping around the small room for a half hour, he changed her into pink footie zip-up pajamas, blowing raspberries on her tummy and eliciting giggles of glee. He tried to lay her in her bed, but she only fussed and clung to him. Sighing, he picked her up and propped himself against the headboard. He didn't really mind the cuddles. She curled up against his chest and sucked contentedly on her pacifier. The ultra-soft, pink teddy bear that she'd always slept with was clutched in her hand and her eyes were already starting to droop.

A memory drew tears to his eyes. A sterile hospital room, machines blinking and beeping in the stillness. Sabrina, oh-so-frail and monitored by so many medical devices, lying in the bed. A too-small Murrae lying on her chest with oxygen prongs in her tiny nose, her bare body covered with a thick hospital blanket. And Tyler curled up next to them, his large frame wedged into the small bed.

They'd been a family for a mere three hours.

Just three hours.

Tyler had gently stroked Sabrina's head, her dark hair thinned and tangled, as his other hand had rested on their daughter's back. He'd tenderly kissed his wife as her breathing grew labored.

And they had lain there.

For what felt like an eternity of time that was still far too short.

Tears trickled down the side of Tyler's face as he dragged himself back to the present with effort. He sniffed, cleared his throat, and rubbed a hand across his face. Stroking Murrae's baby-soft dark curls, he whispered into her tiny ear. "I wish you could have met your mommy . . ."

"Mama?" Murrae drowsily repeated, her head lifting slightly from his shoulder.

"Mama. She was so beautiful and so strong." His voice cracked on the last word, and he inhaled a ragged breath. Tonight was one of those nights—albeit becoming less and less frequent—where the past invaded the present and he felt wrecked by the emotion. They say time heals all wounds, but he was finding time only a lousy painkiller tonight.

Murrae craned her neck to look up at him, and patted his cheek with her tiny palm. "Dada. 'Appy?"

He pressed kisses over her entire face. "Dada's happy. I love you, precious."

She mumbled something and curled back into him, quickly dozing off. Tyler tucked the blanket back over her feet—she always kicked it off—and squeezed his eyes shut, resting his head against the hard headboard.

It had been a year and a half. He shouldn't be crying. He had his daughter. His job. His friends.

Oh, God. Why? It's been eighteen months. But it still hurts. So. Bad. It hurts too much to pray anymore. I can't.

Careful to not jostle Murrae, he reached for his phone on the nightstand. Tucking the earbuds in his ears, he turned his music on loudly enough to drown the painful thoughts.

And he closed his eyes and waited for sleep to lull him into oblivion.

Alyvia shut and locked the door behind her and watched as the headlights of Tyler's truck backed out of the driveway. She was grateful for him taking her home—although she was kind of surprised that Ezra hadn't. Either way, after the wretched evening she'd had, she was just glad to be home. And it was nice to meet Tyler. She'd heard a lot about him from both Piper and Ezra, but she'd only seen him in passing at church some Sundays. She'd met his sweet daughter when Piper had babysat the little girl once.

Alyvia wondered about his wife. Now that she thought about it, she'd never heard anyone mention her. There was a story there, likely. *Not that it's any of my business.*

Turning, she climbed the stairs to her bedroom on the second floor. So much for moving to her new apartment tonight. Her wrist ached—her whole body ached. A hot shower, then an ice pack for her wrist would make her feel a whole lot better.

An hour later, Alyvia climbed into her bed, wet hair pulled into a messy bun, and yoga pants and a comfy tank top on. Tucking the ice pack around her wrist and sighing in relief, she opened her book and started to read.

Finally. Peace and quiet.

Except her brain wasn't cooperating. It drifted, thinking of the bookstore. So much to do. So little time. The roof needed to be patched, if not reshingled. Washington was wet and rainy much of the year, and books and moisture didn't mix well.

After a while, she slammed shut her book and tossed it on the bed, closing her eyes and leaning back, trying to let her mind wander. If there was a problem, her brain wanted to find a solution, even if there wasn't a ready one, and she found herself getting increasingly more tense and stressed. *Think of something else,* she commanded herself.

So she thought about Mrs. Cramer. The poor woman must be terribly lonely. People weren't just incredibly grumpy for no reason.

Her thoughts continued to hopscotch around until sleep finally claimed her, the lamp on the side table still glowing dimly.

Chapter Four

Tyler woke up a few mornings later feeling groggy and grouchy. His arm was numb from lying on it. He laid still for several minutes, digging deep for the motivation to get out of bed. Thank goodness it was a Saturday and he had the weekend off work.

That was one of the most important decisions he made when he returned to work when Murrae was a couple of months old. He had been able to arrange ten-hour day shifts and have at least two days free to spend exclusively with Murrae.

His entire world revolved around the dark-haired, blue-eyed little girl.

Tyler shifted upright and shook out his arm to rid it of the pins-and-needles sensation. He peeked into the portable crib where Murrae still slept peacefully. He adjusted the blanket over her and took advantage of the next half hour to shower, shave, and dress.

He'd gotten the news yesterday that they were finally able to move back into their apartment. The apartment complex and insurance agency had worked surprisingly fast to get everything squared away, and he was grateful. He might go crazy if he had to spend too many more days in this cramped hotel room.

The shower had washed away the grogginess and a cup—or three—of coffee would boost his spirits and his energy level. He slipped a mug underneath the spout and flipped the machine on before turning to wake his daughter. He gently rubbed her back and spoke softly to her. "How's my little 'Rae of sunshine? It's time to get up. Daddy's hungry."

She rubbed her eyes and reached up her arms to be picked up. "'Ungry?" She rested her head on his shoulder as he pulled out a diaper and clean clothes from the suitcase he'd hurriedly packed. Thankfully the smoke hadn't reached the bedroom area of the apartment, so their clothes hadn't been damaged. He quickly changed her and grabbed the hotel key to go down for some breakfast.

Tyler dusted off his hands and heaved a sigh. It was good to be home again. Somehow between chasing Murrae around and keeping the active toddler out of trouble, he was able to put their apartment to rights. The smell of powerful cleaners still lingered in the air, masking the faint bonfire smell, but hopefully that would fade over time. He opened the slider door at the balcony to let the fresh spring air wash into the room.

He stretched his aching back as he watched Murrae playing with her toys on the floor. After however many years as a paramedic, the cramped working space was finally starting to catch up with his tall frame. He was considering chiropractic care if the ache didn't let up soon. But he didn't really have time for that. He didn't have time for much these days.

It was frustrating. Being a single dad was harder than the Hallmark movies made it out to be.

Not that he watched many of those.

"Alrighty, 'Rae, let's get going. Do you wanna go see Ez and Piper and Topher?" He picked her up and tossed her in the air while she jabbered on excitedly, the only discernible word being "Topher." He chuckled. She loved getting to play with the little guy.

Tyler found a light jacket and some shoes for her, as the spring breeze was still a little chilly. Putting her in the baby carrier, he strapped it to his back and locked the apartment door behind him.

He took the stairs to the first floor at a jog and set off at a brisk walk down the street. It was only a ten-minute walk to the main street, and from there just a quick jaunt to the park where they were meeting Ezra, Piper, and their two children for a picnic. It was too beautiful a day to drive.

Tyler allowed his thoughts to wander as he reached the sidewalk at 5th Street. He and Sabrina used to walk to this park every day they could. Just the two of them, holding hands. Chatting about their day. Or just being silent.

Sometimes no words are necessary when you're with your best friend.

He hadn't treasured those days enough. Soon, Sabrina was too weak—and too pregnant—for even a ten-minute walk. And then she was on mandatory bedrest.

And after the birth . . . well, there were no more walks.

Tyler lifted his head and turned the corner only to collide with a body.

Alyvia pushed open the door to Happy Haven Books and barely took two steps onto the sidewalk before a solid form collided with her, sending her and the items in her arms sprawling. She hit the sidewalk with her right hip and shoulder. Though it hurt, her first thought was that she was glad she hadn't landed on her sore wrist. She moaned, more out of frustration than actual pain, as she started to sit up. She looked up to see who knocked her down and met the startled eyes of the paramedic from the other day.

Tyler Collens.

Huh. They needed to stop meeting like this—with her being injured.

Although it was his fault this time around.

He quickly dropped to a knee beside her and reached out a hand. "Alyvia! I am so, so sorry! I wasn't paying attention. Are you okay? Don't move." His shocked, apologetic tone changed to what she guessed was his authoritative, paramedic one.

She waved him off as he reached out to her. "It's okay. I'm fine. Just a bit bruised, not in need of your services." She chuckled at her own joke, but he still looked concerned.

"Are you sure? I feel terrible. I wasn't even paying attention." He looked so remorseful it was kind of cute. She frowned at the thought.

"No, no, really. It's okay. I wouldn't mind a hand up, though."

"Of course." He stood, grabbing her good hand and pulling her up. Then frowned as he glanced about the sidewalk. Her backpack, two books, and a few random papers littered it. "I'm sorry about your stuff, too." He bent to pick everything up before she had a chance to and handed the items to her.

"Don't even worry about it," she said with a smile. A baby jabbered off a string of dialogue, and Alyvia caught sight of the baby carrier on his back. "You have Murrae with you?" She stepped behind Tyler before he had a chance to respond. "Well, hello, cutie! It's been a while, huh?" She caught the baby's hand as Murrae grinned at her from the carrier on her daddy's back.

Tyler glanced over his shoulder and chuckled as he stuck his hands in his jeans pockets. "So, you two have met?"

"Of course! We're old friends, aren't we, sweetheart?" she cooed to the baby. Then she stopped, suddenly embarrassed. Tyler turned around. "We've met at Piper's house," she explained.

Tyler nodded. "Ah. Piper has been kind enough to watch Murrae for me when my usual nanny can't."

She nodded, and the following silence grew awkward.

Finally, Tyler shuffled his feet and cleared his throat. "So, um. Murrae and I are meeting Piper and Ezra and the kids at the park on the corner for a picnic. You'd be more than welcome to come. Uh, that is, if you don't have anything else going on. I mean, I'm sure you're probably busy." He rubbed the back of his neck with an almost-wince.

She laughed. "That's funny, I was just headed there. Mind if I walk with you?"

He gestured down the sidewalk. "I'd be offended if you didn't. After you."

"All right. Just let me put my stuff in my car."

They reached the park and quickly spotted the Bryants. Piper sat at a picnic table with baby Haevyn, watching as Ezra chased a screaming Christopher in circles around another table.

"Hey, guys! Look who I found." Tyler waved a hand dramatically at Alyvia. Piper stood up and grinned when she saw her friend and gave her a hug. Ezra swooped up Topher and tickled his belly, eliciting giggles from the little boy as they walked over to join them.

"Hey, Alyvia. Good to see you. How are you feeling?" Ezra asked with a smile.

"Pretty good, thanks. That is, until Tyler literally knocked me over." She sent him a look, but he noticed she was smiling.

He cringed anyway. "I'm sor—"

Alyvia laughed, cutting him off. "I'm just teasing."

Piper looked curiously between the two of them. "What happened?"

Alyvia grinned at him as she spoke. "Well, I was just minding my own business, locking up the store. When I stepped out onto the sidewalk—"

Piper cut in. "Let me guess—you were knocked over by the Hulk himself?"

They all chuckled at the apt description. It wasn't the first time he'd been called such. "Pretty much. I'm so sorry, Aly—" Tyler started to apologize again, but Alyvia stopped him.

"Really. It's okay. It was an accident."

Piper and Alyvia walked back to the picnic table and started cooing over the baby. Tyler turned toward Ezra and reached to take off the baby carrier that Murrae still peacefully occupied. Ezra looked at him and raised his brows, sliding his hands into his jeans pockets.

"Bumped into her, huh. Convenient." Ezra smirked.

Tyler paused, confused. Then he gave a scowl-shrug and pulled Murrae out of the wrap, annoyed at his friend's insinuation. "Very funny, Ez. Now knock it off."

Ezra raised his hands, palms out. "What? I'm halfway serious. That *is* convenient."

Tyler sat Murrae in the grass at his feet, where she happily started pulling up handfuls of grass and dropping them on her head. She'd need a bath later. "I'd concede your point if I happened to be interested in . . . any of that." He waved a hand in the air. "But I'm not."

Shrugging, Ezra looked down at Murrae. "But you could be. It's been nearly two years, man. Sometime—"

Tyler sent an annoyed glance toward Ezra, but didn't trust himself enough to make eye contact. "Don't. Just don't. Two years or not, you can't just expect me to forget and move on. It doesn't work like that. Murrae, no!" He reached down to rescue a grasshopper from being the little girl's dinner.

Ezra sighed. "I didn't mean it like that, Ty. Don't you think I know it doesn't work like that? Because I do. Nobody is asking you to forget." He paused and stared toward the playground where Alyvia was pushing Topher on the swings. "But you do have to say goodbye sometime, man," he added softly.

Tyler couldn't meet his friend's eyes for the pain swirling behind his own. He forced an evenness into his tone that he didn't feel. "Maybe. But even so, I'm not there yet."

Ezra nodded, seeming content to let the subject drop, and Tyler was grateful. They both were silent for a few moments, watching as Murrae wandered around, chasing yellow dandelions. Finally, Ezra shifted and pulled his hands out of his pockets. "Well, how about dinner?" He leaned down to grab the little girl's hand and lead her toward the others. "You hungry, Murrae? Huh?" After two kids, Ezra had the higher-pitched dad voice down to a T. It made Tyler chuckle as he followed Ezra and his daughter at a slower pace toward the picnic tables where Piper was setting out the food, Haevyn cocooned in a cloth wrap at her chest. Tyler watched as Ezra popped a grape in Murrae's eager mouth, then leaned in to kiss his wife.

His heart twisted at the sight. That used to be him.

Tyler sighed. Some days were worse than others, but his conversation with Ezra had made today one of those harder days. He knew the man was well-meaning. But it still stung like an irritating bee.

He plastered a smile on his face and strode over to join the group.

Chapter Five

"So, Alyvia, how's work at the bookstore going?" Piper asked as they sat around the picnic table, devouring sub sandwiches, chips, and fruit. The April air was cooling as dusk settled in, but it was still warm enough to be comfortable as the sun met the horizon.

Alyvia paused at the question and put the chip she was about to eat back on her plate. "Well." She grinned somewhat sheepishly. "Are you sure you want to ask?"

Piper smiled. "That bad?"

Alyvia shook her head and popped the chip into her mouth. "My to-do list terrifies me so much I can't even look at it," she said around the crunch.

"Oh boy. Do you need help?"

Taking a sip out of her soda can, she set it back down on the wooden picnic table before answering. "I do. But the thing is, I don't even know where to start."

Piper nodded, bouncing Haevyn gently with one hand while munching on a carrot stick in the other. "Can you prioritize? Figure out what *needs* to get done first, and make a list from there. Some of the bigger things—like a roof repair—you may not be able to start right away, so then pick something smaller. If you work on it little by little, it won't be so overwhelming."

Alyvia nodded as she chewed, absorbing the wisdom of her friend's words. She had a good point—the only thing better than to-do lists was prioritized to-do lists.

"And—" Piper leaned forward, making eye contact with the look on her face that Alyvia had seen her use when she wanted her three-year-old son to listen carefully to her. "Ask for help, okay? It's no crime. If you try to tackle all this alone, you'll find yourself buried quicker than you can snap your fingers. Independence looks more like loneliness after a while. Trust me, I'd know."

Alyvia chuckled. "Duly noted. Aren't you just full of wisdom tonight?"

Piper tilted her head and raised her eyebrows, a slight smile on her lips. "Spoken in love, as always. You know I'm right."

"You're not wrong, I'll concede that," Alyvia said, folding her arms and leaning on the table.

Her friend rolled her eyes with a slight shake of her head. "Always have to have the last word, don't you?"

Alyvia tilted her soda can toward Piper with a grin before taking a sip.

For the next half hour they sat around the picnic table, the conversation bouncing between random topics among the four adults, frequently interrupted by the children. Eventually, the sun began to head below the horizon and the street lights flickered on.

"Thanks for tonight, guys. I needed this." Alyvia directed a smile toward Piper, and they all nodded in agreement.

"Anytime." Piper smiled and stood. "Show your face around the house a little more frequently, all right?" Alyvia nodded with a grateful smile, and Piper turned to her husband. "We need to get home, Ezra." She motioned to Topher, lying asleep on the bench next to his dad.

Alyvia hugged Piper and the little family said their goodbyes. They headed to their car, Topher still sleeping, now on Ezra's shoulder.

Alyvia turned back to the table as Tyler stood up, Murrae sleeping on his shoulder as well.

"Come on. I'll walk you to your car." He gestured down the sidewalk with the hand not holding his daughter.

"Oh, you don't have to."

He laughed quietly. "Well, it's literally on my way home, so I don't think you can avoid me."

"Oh." She bit her cheek, slightly embarrassed that she hadn't realized the obvious. Sometimes she felt so dense. They started across the park toward the sidewalk, and she looked up as Tyler shifted Murrae in his arms. "Can I carry her?"

He looked down at her. "She's heavy."

"That's okay. I want to."

He shrugged and shifted the sleeping girl to Alyvia's shoulder. The baby sighed and snuggled closer, and Alyvia felt herself melting. She gently stroked the little girl's back as they started walking again.

Tyler tucked his hands in his pockets as they headed down the sidewalk. Alyvia looked cute with Murrae.

He scratched the back of his neck, suddenly uncomfortable. Why would he even think that?

The peaceful night sounds of crickets chirping and quiet traffic noises filled the silent airwaves between them, and he didn't feel the need to compound it with chatter. Nor did she, apparently. When they reached her car, he held out his arms to take Murrae. Alyvia lifted the little girl from her shoulder and just as Tyler gripped her, Alyvia's arm buckled under the weight of the twenty-some-pound toddler.

"How's your wrist doing?" he asked as he cradled Murrae in the crook of his arm.

She shook her head, simultaneously shaking out her wrist. "It's much better—just a tiny bit sore."

He nodded. "That's good. You should probably wrap it again when you get home."

Grinning, she tilted her head back to look at him. "Do you often give others unsolicited medical advice?" she asked, reaching out to stroke a finger across the little girl's cheek.

Tyler froze, feeling his face get warm. Then he gave a sheepish grin. "Sorry. Job hazard, I guess you could say. You couldn't take the medic out of me if you tried."

"I guess." She laughed, then paused. "Well, take care, Tyler."

He suddenly felt reluctant to go home to his quiet apartment—but his arm was getting sore from holding Murrae's dead weight. "You too, Alyvia." He reached out and opened her car door for her.

She smiled her thanks and climbed in, but he hesitated before closing the door, and she looked up at him. "Hey . . . I couldn't help but overhear you and Piper talking earlier. If you need some help with your bookstore, just let me know. I'm not really doing anything but being at the munchkin's beck and call most weeknights," he said with a laugh.

Seeming surprised, she studied him for a second. "That's nice of you, Tyler, but I couldn't ask that."

"But you didn't, right? I offered." He gave his best charming grin.

She laughed softly. "Fair enough, I guess. I may take you up on that. Thanks."

He nodded. "G'night, Alyvia." He firmly closed her door as her "good night" drifted out. Lifting a hand in a wave as he turned, he started down the sidewalk, following the streetlights around the corner.

Alyvia Emmerson was an anomaly. He looked down at his daughter. "But she's nice, isn't she, 'Rae?" The little girl, smelling of grass and fresh air, was zonked. A bath could wait until tomorrow. He smiled as he climbed the stairs to his apartment. It had been a good evening.

Chapter Six

Alyvia padded down the stairs to the kitchen and headed straight for the Keurig. Perks of living with your coffee-loving mother: a fancy coffee maker. The plan was to finally move into the apartment above the bookstore today. She would have to buy her own coffee maker then, as she didn't think her mom would appreciate her stealing the Keurig.

She had the house to herself because her mom was still in Seattle visiting her first grandson, Maddison's baby boy. Thankfully, her brothers, Micah and Aaron, had agreed to help her move her things. The convenience of brothers—built-in laborers.

She grabbed her mug from under the spout of the coffee machine and paused to inhale the earthy scent before taking a sip—and burning her tongue. "Ouch! You'd think I'd learn . . ." she muttered to herself as she grabbed a sweet croissant from the pantry. A healthy breakfast, it was not.

Alyvia sat down at the dining table and pulled up the Kindle app on her phone to her current read. Peaceful morning before the busyness of the day.

A door slammed and startled her, causing her coffee to slosh. She growled in frustration and mopped the liquid up with a nearby dish rag. Thudding footsteps entered the kitchen behind her, followed by the bang of cabinet doors closing.

Sometimes she wondered why Micah's fiancée, Natalie, had agreed to marry him.

"Good morning, Micah," she said sardonically without turning around as she took a bite of her croissant.

There was a brief pause. "Oh, hi, Lyv. Didn't know you were there," her brother answered.

"Obviously." She turned to grin at him. "Can't you enter someone's residence without waking the whole neighborhood? You're lucky I was already awake or you might have received a less pleasant good morning."

Micah's green eyes danced as he laughed. "Sorry about that. I honestly thought you would already be at the shop." He pulled a muffin out of a container in the pantry. Knowing her children as well as she did, their mother kept the household well stocked in baked goods.

"It's a Saturday, Micah."

He paused, a muffin in each hand and a bite already in his mouth. "Oh. Forgot," he mumbled through the crumbs.

Alyvia just shook her head. Micah was the "pretty one" of the family, but he was also a bit absentminded

46

and hopelessly nerdy. He bore the brunt of the family's teasing for it, but she loved the quirkiness of her brother's personality. They were the closest in age and had been nearly inseparable growing up.

"You didn't forget you and Aaron were going to help me move this morning, did you?"

Micah came and sat beside her at the table and shot her another grin. Alyvia set aside her phone. "No. Why do you think I'm here?"

She raised an eyebrow at him. "Because there's food."

He shrugged. "That too."

She shook her head again with a chuckle. They both munched on their breakfasts in silence for a few moments until Micah cleared his throat. She looked up.

"How're you doing, Lyv?"

She frowned at the candid question. "Not bad. Why do you ask?"

Micah gave another one-shouldered shrug. "Just wondering. You seem a little different lately."

Alyvia ate the last bite of her croissant. "Oh. Well, I'm just busy and a bit stressed figuring out this whole 'run a bookstore' thing. It's harder than I thought." She smiled wryly.

Micah nodded slowly as he took another bite, then pressed his fingertips against the table to pick up the crumbs left behind. "No other reason then?"

Alyvia frowned and tilted her head, trying to make eye contact, but her brother still stared at the table. "Micah. Why are you equivocating?"

Now he looked up at her, eyebrows raised. "If I knew what that meant, I might tell you." He smirked.

She rolled her eyes. "Ambiguous. Evasive. Oblique. Cryptic."

"Oh. I'm not doing any of that."

She sent him a look. He sighed and caved, placing both palms flat on the table and leaning back. "Look, does any of this," he waved a hand indirectly at her, "general turmoil I sense from you in the past few weeks have anything to do with Dad?"

Now Alyvia leaned back and refrained from folding her arms. "What do you mean?" she hedged.

Micah sighed—again. "Listen. Now who's being evasive? You haven't been yourself. I've noticed it. Mom's noticed it. Dad—"

"What'd Dad say?" she interrupted.

"Nothing. But, Lyv, you gotta see the man is trying. Isn't that worth something?"

She shrugged and pushed her chair back to stand. "We'll see. Hey, I've just got a few more things to put in boxes, then I'll be ready to go." She turned toward the staircase to the second floor and called over her shoulder, "When's Aaron going to be here?"

Even from halfway across the house, she could sense her brother's frustration, and he didn't bother to answer her question. He'd always been the fix-it man in the family and she imagined this conversation wasn't over. But it was for now. He wasn't her parent, and she didn't have to have this discussion if she didn't want to.

But as she threw the last random things left in her room into a large cardboard box, she was aware that she was avoiding the subject because Micah was probably right. "But today is not the day to deal with this," she muttered to herself. "Because today is the day you are finally moving to the store!" She punctuated each word with the closing of a flap on the box, then turned and retraced her steps back down the stairs.

Micah was waiting at the bottom, texting, but he put his phone in his pocket as she came down. She started to slip by him, but he reached out and slipped his arm around her neck and tugged her to him, playfully using a fist to muss her hair. She winced.

"We're going to finish this conversation later, kiddo. Got it?"

"Yeah, yeah, now let me go." She pushed against him, but his chest was firm muscle.

He slid his arms lower over her shoulders into a gentle hug that she stopped fighting. "I love you, Lyv. 'Kay?"

Her smile was hidden in his chest. "'Kay."

Micah pushed her away from him. "'Kay'? Just 'kay'?"

She laughed, then punched his arm. "I love you too, you big lug. Now where's Aaron?"

"I don't know, but if he's this late, he better have brought donuts."

On cue, the front door slammed. Did none of her brothers know how to close a door? "Did someone say donuts?" Aaron walked into the foyer, carrying a white box aloft, the logo of their favorite bakery on the sides.

"Dude!" Micah nabbed the box. "You can be late any day."

"Hey, hey, treats after you work," Alyvia said as she gave Aaron a quick hug. "Boxes are upstairs. Let's move!" She clapped her hands briskly, then grabbed the donut box from Micah as he started to open it. He sent her a glare, but both brothers started up the stairs.

She set the box of donuts on the table and paused to smile. I-love-yous were rare among her siblings. She knew they all thought it, but they rarely said it—they didn't have to.

Turning, she followed the sound of male laughter back up the steps.

Chapter Seven

"Unit three, we have a report of a six-year-old female with a potential wrist fracture." The dispatcher gave the address. "Are you able to respond?"

Tyler picked up the radio mic. "Copy. We're five out." He put the rig in gear and pulled out onto the street.

"Copy that. Teenage sister called it in. She said the parents aren't home. I have a squad unit on the way; they'll attempt to locate the parents."

"Roger."

They quickly arrived at the small, sad-looking house in one of the worst parts of downtown. Ezra keyed his shoulder radio as Ty grabbed the medic bags.

"ETA on the cops?"

"About another five minutes."

"Copy that." Ezra took his finger off the radio button. "Let's go, partner."

As they reached the worn red door, it swung open, revealing a girl in her mid-teens, her mascara causing black tear rivulets down her flushed cheeks. Without a word, she turned and gestured them into the house. Ezra glanced at Tyler as they followed her through the living room and kitchen to a back room. The house was a mess and reeked of stale food and alcohol.

The teen led them to a bedroom where a young girl sat on the bed, clutching her arms to herself with her head down. She looked up as they entered, and Tyler absorbed the sight of the small, heart-shaped face with almond eyes and delicate features. His chest ached at the sight of her split lip and swollen jaw. He met Ezra's eyes, and he nodded. His partner depressed the button on his radio and began a murmured dialogue with the dispatcher.

"Dispatch, what's the current ETA on the squad car? I think we're looking at a domestic violence case here. It might be good to have social services on the line . . ."

Tyler stepped to the bed and knelt in front of the girl. "Hey there, sweetheart. My name is Ty, and I want to help you. Is that okay?" he asked in a gentle voice. He opened the red medic bag and pulled on a pair of disposable gloves, making eye contact and visually assessing the girl's condition as he did so.

She looked up behind him at her sister questioningly, and must have gotten a confirmation, as she nodded at him.

"Can you tell me your name?"

"Lilah," she whispered.

"That's a pretty name." He smiled at her, but her face remained solemn, tears slowly tracking down her smudged face. His gut clenched as anger surged at the person responsible for the somberness in eyes that said they'd seen too much. She was so little. "All right, Lilah, I think your mouth must hurt, but does anywhere else hurt?"

She stared at him for a moment, as if deciding whether she could trust him with her injuries. Then she looked down at her right arm.

Tyler pulled a small air splint out of the bag and set it on the bed next to him. "Okay, Lilah. I'm going to check your heartbeat in your arm, okay?" She looked confused as with gentle fingers he took her uninjured wrist and felt for a pulse. Steady, if on the fast side. Her breathing seemed to be okay for now, although he could see the pain on her face.

He carefully explained each step of his process to her as he splinted her wrist and dabbed at the blood on her face with gauze. As he did so, he could hear Ezra alternately conversing with the teen and dispatch. After he stabilized Lilah's arm, he gently moved her to the stretcher, where she curled up into a ball on her side, crying now, but completely silent. Each silent shudder that wracked her body tore at his heart.

He hated this part of his job.

Taking advantage of her position on her side, he placed the bell of his stethoscope on her upper back and moved it across. Then frowned at the uneven breath sounds. He'd missed something. Gently, he braced her tiny body and rolled her onto her back, then tugged up the hem of her grimy shirt. An ugly dark bruise stained the right side of her lower rib cage.

Tyler turned to his partner. "Ez, we need to transport. Where are the cops?"

"Should be here any second." A door slammed. "That'd be them. What do we have going on?" Ezra came around to the other side of the stretcher as Tyler slid an oxygen mask over Lilah's face as her breathing became more labored and her still-silent sobs increased. He started to fill Ezra in. "Likely fracture of the right radius, may have a fractured rib or two on the left side with potential internal—" A loud yell cut him off, and he whipped around to be met with a hefty, well-placed fist to his temple that knocked him sideways.

The world blurred to black.

Someone was yelling. It resounded like a thousand tiny jackhammers in his head. Tyler groaned and blinked open his eyes. The world slowly swam into focus.

"Welcome back, brother." Ezra's voice.

What the heck?" He groaned again and assessed his position. He was lying prone on smelly, scratchy carpet.

"The girls' dad showed up, and I'm afraid he wasn't too happy to see us. Unfortunately, you took the brunt of his wrath."

"Yeah, I remember that part with great clarity. You're welcome. Sheesh, aren't they going to shut him up?" He flung his arm across his eyes to shut out the light and noise.

Ezra pulled Tyler's arm off his head. "He's in the cops' hands on charges of child abuse and assault." He shined a penlight in Tyler's eyes, and Tyler winced.

"Ow." Then he shot straight up. "Lilah!" He groaned and clutched his head at the sharp pain the sudden movement brought on. Ezra pushed him back down.

"Take it easy there, partner. That wasn't just a little conk on the head. That dude was massive. Lilah's fine and on her way to the hospital with her sister. You seem about as coherent as you ever are, but your pupils are a bit sluggish. What's your middle name and date of birth?"

Tyler purposefully hesitated and frowned. Ezra leaned over him, humor replaced by concern on his face. "Ty?"

He chuckled, then stopped when it sent more hammers to his head. "Kidding. Levi, ten-twenty-two-eighty-eight."

His friend glared at him. "Idiot. Just for that, you're getting a ride in the bus."

"Nuh-uh. You can't make me. I'm fine. You're the one who says I have a hard head. Now help me up. This carpet stinks."

Ezra sighed, grabbed his hand, and pulled him to a sitting position. Tyler squinted through the dizziness. "Whoaaa. So this is a concussion?"

"Fun, right? Try a TBI." Ezra had suffered a traumatic brain injury several years ago that had left him in a coma for five days, so Tyler imagined he knew what he was feeling right now. "I won't make you ride in the back of the bus, but you are going to be seen by an ER doc." Tyler started to argue, but Ezra held a hand up, palm out. "Don't whine about it or I will make you ride in the back, restraints and all."

Tyler groaned, but allowed his friend to pull him to his feet. After the room mostly stopped moving, he shook off Ezra's grip and started for the door. He made it to the passenger side of the ambulance and winced as he hauled himself up. A few officers followed him and he heard Ezra convincing them to wait until later to talk with him.

Ezra climbed into the driver's seat and started the engine. "Doing all right?"

Tyler leaned his aching head back against the seat and closed his eyes. "Just awesome." He formed the okay sign by pinching together his index finger and thumb.

"If you say so, Rambo. Sirens?"

"Don't you dare."

Tyler shouldered out of the heavy ER doors and headed out into the parking lot, squinting at the bright sunlight that pierced his eyes. His normal good humor had been replaced with sheer annoyance. "Mild concussion—I could have diagnosed that. This was such a waste of time. I could have been home with Murrae for several hours already." Thankfully his injury had occurred at the end of the day, so he wouldn't lose any hours. The department had already issued a mandatory two-day leave, and he couldn't afford to cut back on his hours any more. He spotted his blue F-150 in the side lot—courtesy of his cop buddy, Jeff—and angled toward it.

Ezra, trailing behind him, must have just decided to let him whine, as he didn't say anything.

Yes, he was whining, but this was not how he'd wanted his week to go.

"Count it all joy when you fall into various trials, I guess," he muttered under his breath. Those painkillers were for the birds. His head still raged. He pulled open the door to his truck and nabbed the keys from under the driver's side carpet. "Thank you, Jeff," he muttered. He started to haul himself in, but a firm hand clamped on his shoulder.

"Ah ah, nice try."

Tyler stopped and closed his eyes. "Oh, come *on*, Ez. I can drive."

"You can, but you may not. Get in the passenger seat."

Tyler turned to face his friend. "I—"

Ezra gave him a fierce glare that stopped his words. "Listen up, bud, 'cause I'm only gonna say this once. *I* am driving you to your place, where we'll pick up Murrae. Then I am taking you home where Piper will cook you a nice dinner, and there's a couch with your name on it where I can wake your grumpy self up every two hours as the doctor said. And tomorrow afternoon, *if* you feel better, you can go home. Mild or not, you don't mess with head injuries. Got it?" At the end of his tirade, Ezra held out his hand for the keys, which Tyler dropped in his palm. Apparently Ezra had reached the end of his good humor, too. Or he was tired of Tyler's complaining. He *had* been griping . . . a lot.

He felt like a whipped puppy dog. He rounded the front of the truck and climbed into the passenger seat. Ezra started the truck and turned the radio down. Tyler chewed on the inside of his lip in the silence. As Ezra pulled out onto the street, he let out a sigh.

"Look. I'm sorry if I seem frustrated. You just don't listen sometimes, and I wanted to get my point across. I don't think you're taking this seriously enough."

Tyler leaned his head back and blew out a breath of frustration. "It's a mild concussion." He stressed the descriptor.

"Mild, yes. But you feel miserable, don't you?"

Tyler didn't answer.

"My point exactly. Now stop being stubborn and take two of those painkillers the doc gave you."

"I already did. They don't work," he mumbled, then reclined his seat back and closed his eyes. He felt guilty for being short with Ezra, but his headache was too violent to form a cohesive apology. Or so he told himself. *It's just been a lot lately, okay, God? I could use a break.* By the time he opened his eyes again, Ezra was pulling in the driveway of the small home he and his wife shared.

"I've got Murrae," Ezra said as he climbed out of the truck. Tyler decided to not even bother with a nod, even though his headache had calmed to a dull roar in the back of his head. Maybe those painkillers actually did work. He felt his temple as he swung his legs out of the vehicle. Yep. Definitely a nice goose egg. He followed Ezra to the door, Murrae lying sleepily on his friend's shoulder. It was past her bedtime, and Tyler wanted to cuddle his baby.

Piper smiled at them from the kitchen as they entered. "Hey, guys. Go ahead and sit down, and I'll get you something to eat. I'll grab an ice pack for your head, too, Tyler."

"Thanks, Piper, I'd appreciate it." Actually, he was somewhat nauseated, but he knew he needed to eat something. He pulled Murrae from Ezra's arms and sank onto the couch.

"Dada." Murrae pulled out her pacifier and smiled at him.

He grinned back at her. "Hey, baby girl."

Her lips puckered and she reached toward his head. "Dada owie?"

He flinched as her tiny finger poked more firmly than he expected. "It's just a baby owie. Tiny." He captured her fingers that reached toward his head again and kissed them.

"Tiny?" she repeated.

"Yup."

Seeming satisfied, she cuddled up on his chest, and Tyler leaned his head back on the couch cushion. He heard Ezra and Piper speaking in hushed tones in the kitchen, then a door shut and Ezra handed him an ice pack. He thanked him and placed it against his forehead, wincing at the sting of the cold. Murrae fell asleep in his arms, and Piper took her into the room where their kids were already sleeping and a porta-crib had been set up for her. It was nearly 9:30 before he and Ezra finished eating. Tyler sank back onto the couch and replaced the slushy ice pack on his head. "You guys got any decent sports channels?" he asked, flipping through the channels, hoping for a distraction.

The little girl's face wouldn't leave him. Lilah. Her obsidian eyes, so bright yet dulled by pain, looking too large in the dusky, smooth skin of her face. There was no bright sparkle of imagination and joy he saw often in Murrae's. Just . . . a maturity born of too much pain too soon.

No one should have to experience that at such a young age. No one should have to experience that at *any* age.

This was by no means his first domestic violence callout . . . but it hit him in an already bruised place. "Do you know anything about Lilah?" he asked quietly, staring at the TV, but not seeing it.

Ezra looked up and considered him for a moment. "The little girl? No, not really. She stabilized but was admitted. They were able to track down the mother, and she was with her."

Tyler nodded and changed the channel. *It feels so heavy right now, God. I can't keep carrying this.*

Then give it to me, came the answer.

"You okay, Tyler?"

He looked up and saw Piper watching him, standing behind Ezra's chair, her arms around his neck. He forced a chuckle and pointed to his head. "Concussion, remember? It hurts."

Piper smiled but gave him a look that said she didn't quite believe that was all. Intuitive, she was.

"You should get some sleep. I'll grab an extra pillow and blanket."

"Thanks, Ma." The grin he gave her took the sting out of the sarcasm, and Ezra chuckled.

Tyler mindlessly flipped through the channels as he felt his body relax and exhaustion pull on him. His eyelids closed and the next thing he knew, a hand was nudging his shoulder. Out of reflex, he pushed it away, and rolled over.

And thudded hard onto the floor. He groaned and clutched his head. The jarring had reawakened the latent headache.

"You okay, Ty?"

Oh. Ezra. Ezra's house. Ezra's couch. Ezra's tiny couch; that thing was not made for his large frame. "I'm great," he said as he hauled himself back onto the couch and scrubbed a hand across his face, the stubble on his chin scratchy. "What day is it?" He glanced around the still dark room.

"It's one a.m."

"Aw, shoot. I was hoping you weren't actually going to wake me up."

"Ha. You know better than that."

"Yeah, I do, unfortunately. Now let me go back to sleep." He swung his legs back onto the couch and pulled the blanket around himself.

Ezra slapped his shoulder lightly and moved away, then came back with an ice pack.

Tyler took it and placed it on his head. "Thanks, Dad. I haven't felt this much like a nine-year-old in twenty-one years."

His friend chuckled quietly. "No problem, son. Now go back to sleep."

Chapter Eight

Tyler pushed open the door to Happy Haven Books and the scent of books, coffee, and . . . something floral wafted toward him. A walk with Murrae to get some fresh air had helped clear his head; the pain still vibrated through his skull, but it was more a manageable ache than the roar it had been. He wasn't really sure why he found himself at the bookstore . . . Somehow his feet had led him here without him even realizing it.

Traitorous feet.

He glanced around the mostly empty store, catching sight of Alyvia behind the counter, her nose buried in a crisp hardback.

He cleared his throat. "Alyvia?"

She jumped up so quickly her rolling chair scooted backward and hit the wall behind the desk. "Tyler!" She cleared her throat. "I didn't hear you come in."

Tucking a napkin between the pages of her book, she set it aside and leaned her forearms on the counter.

An amused smile found its way to his face. "Apparently."

"The bell must be broken," she said as she came around the desk and reached up on tiptoes to shake the bell attached to the door frame—although he distinctly remembered hearing it ring when he walked in. It jingled as she touched it, and she paused before turning to him with a shrug and a small, sheepish smile. "So, how are you doing? Hi, Murrae!" She gave the little girl a wide smile. "Can I have a hug, pumpkin?" She held out her arms, and Murrae lunged into them with a babbled, "'Ello!"

Tyler chuckled as Murrae wrapped her arms tightly around Alyvia's neck. The little girl was so free with her affection; it was adorable. He might have to deal with that in fifteen years if that was still the case, though. "I'm all right. How 'bout you?"

Alyvia looked up at him with a smile. "I'm doing pretty well. Whoaaa, what happened to your head?" Concern crossed her face as she spotted the no doubt black-and-blue bump on his temple—now more of a chicken egg than a goose egg, thankfully. Her fingers reached toward it, but stopped halfway.

His lips quirked. "It's fine. All in a day's work."

"But what happened? Did you hit your head?" She stared at it for a moment before meeting his eyes.

He shook his head and tucked his fingers into his jeans pockets.

Alyvia looked at Murrae. "Murrae, what did Daddy do to himself? Did he get an owie?"

Murrae pulled her finger from her mouth and pointed it at him, her face solemn. "Dada owie."

Alyvia looked up at him again, her face sharper. "Did someone hit you?" Her brow wrinkled. "Ezra? Did you get into a fight?"

He burst out laughing—which awakened the sleeping beast in his head. "No!" He gave her a look. "Can you even picture Ezra ever hitting someone?"

Alyvia grinned then and shook her head. "Are you going to tell me what happened or not?"

He spread his hands. "It's just not that big of a deal. This dude was just a little too slap-happy with his fists—and he used me as a demonstration. But he won't be using them on anyone again. At least for a few years." His jaw clenched, spiking a pain into his head, and he felt the anger grow in his voice at the mention of a man who would beat innocent little girls.

Alyvia was quiet for a moment. "I'm sorry, Tyler," she said softly.

"Me too." He took a deep breath. "Anyway," he waved a hand and glanced around, "show me around this place Piper keeps talking about so much. It looks . . . nice."

Alyvia laughed. "It looks like any other bookstore to you, doesn't it?"

He shrugged, affecting a wounded air. "I can tell a nice bookstore when I see one."

"Uh-huh. Sorry, but you don't look like the bookish type," she teased.

"Oh, wow, so wouldn't that be considered judging a book by its cover?"

65

She laughed again. "Touché."

"I can't say you're wrong, but Murrae likes books, don't'cha, 'Rae?" He looked at his daughter who waved a hand and jabbered off a string of sounds, the only decipherable word being "book."

"See?"

Alyvia laughed. "Well, let me see what I can do. Come on, sweetie. Let's go find a book." She turned and walked toward a corner of the store that had brightly colored walls and bookshelves.

He had to smile at the sight the two of them made. Clearly, his daughter was quite fond of Alyvia. *They say children are the best judges of character* . . . He wasn't sure where that thought was leading.

Tyler hadn't noticed he'd lagged behind, but he picked up his pace and reached the children's section. Alyvia and Murrae sat on a soft, brightly colored rug, several picture books lying on the floor between them. Alyvia held a book so the little girl could see the pictures and was teaching her to be gentle with the pages.

Sinking onto a beanbag that was far closer to the floor than he'd anticipated, he laughed as Murrae petted the page of the book and said "gentle," a new concept they'd been working on. Alyvia laughed as well. "Yes. Good job, girlie."

At those words, Murrae looked up at him with a giant cheesy grin and clapped, then joined in on the adults' laughter.

"She's a smart little thing," Alyvia commented, still sitting cross-legged on the floor and watching as Murrae toddled toward the toy bin in the corner.

"Yeah, well, she certainly doesn't get it from me," Tyler joked. "That's all her mother's genes." He smiled and found that the mention of her didn't hurt like it usually did. Alyvia laughed lightly.

They both watched as Murrae pulled items from the bin, analyzing each toy before setting it down carefully and moving on to the next.

"So, any progress on your to-do list?" Tyler asked, the too-small bean bag chair shifting underneath him.

Alyvia half rolled her eyes and shook her head. "Not as much as I would like. But it's a start."

A bell rang from the front of the store, signaling a customer.

She hopped up. "Be right back."

Tyler looked over at Murrae and found her tugging at the page of a book. He reached for her hand. "Be gentle, 'Rae. Don't rip it."

She looked up. "Gen'le?"

"Yeah." He smiled.

Alyvia returned a few minutes later and dropped back down to the floor.

"What's left on your list?" he asked, wanting to keep the conversation going, even though he knew it was getting close to Murrae's naptime.

"The roof is leaking in several spots, the bathroom needs a new sink, bookshelves need fixing . . . I'm not really sure how I'm going to be able to do it all. But I'm going to give it my best shot." She smiled up at him, clearly optimistic despite the daunting tasks.

"I'll help." Wait, what? The words had left his mouth before he'd even thought about them. What was he thinking? He already had enough on his plate—

"Really?" Alyvia looked so relieved and excited, he couldn't have said no if he wanted to . . . not that he wanted to. He was terrible at telling people no.

"Sure. Make a list of what needs doing, and I'll come over a couple nights a week, maybe a Saturday."

"Tyler, that would be . . . amazing. But . . ." She bit her lip and looked at her lap before looking up with a wince. "I can't pay you."

He snorted. "As if I'd let you. Don't even worry about it. I'm just a friend helping a friend. Besides, I enjoy working with my hands." He held them up.

She looked relieved. "Thanks, Tyler. I'd really appreciate it."

He found himself grinning pleased at the prospect of "being a friend." "Like I said, don't worry about it. Now, I better get a little miss home for a nap," he said, nodding toward the corner where Murrae looked as if she were about to doze off. "Thanks for letting us drop by."

"Of course! I'm glad you did. Have a good rest of your day. Bye, Murrae!" She waved at her, and Murrae gave a sleepy "bye" back while rubbing her eyes. Alyvia chuckled. "See ya, Tyler."

"In a while, crocodile." He waved over his shoulder as he headed toward the door.

Chapter Nine

Tyler strode through the familiar sliding front doors of Cascade Valley Hospital and angled toward the front desk. He leaned his crossed forearms on the counter and grinned at the older woman who looked up and started when she noticed him.

"Why, Margaret, I must say, you are looking as lovely as ever today."

Margaret flushed slightly and rolled her eyes. "Now, Tyler, what have I told you about flirting with the female members of the staff? You're going to get yourself in trouble sometime."

"Me? In trouble? Aw, come on, Margie, you know everyone loves me." He sent her a wink and color suffused her face again. "And how are you doing today?"

An amused smile tilted her lips as she folded her hands on the desk and looked up to meet his eyes. "I'm doing fine, thank you. And yourself?"

"Good, all good." He straightened. "Hey, do you know where I might find Cecile?" he asked, referring to the nurse manager.

"What? You mean you didn't just come here to see me? Why, now I'm offended."

Tyler contained the grin and pulled his most serious face and tone, leaning against the desk again and making eye contact. "Margaret. You know I *always* come here to see you. It's the highlight of my day!"

Margaret laughed and waved him off. "Oh, go on with you, you little flirt." She gave him directions to find the nurse manager.

He grinned and blew her a kiss as he backed away from the desk. "You're the best, Marg. Have a fabulous day."

He pushed through the door leading deeper into the hospital, leaving the older woman chuckling and rolling her eyes at his antics. Striding purposefully down the corridor, he quickly spotted the nurse manager, known by most as Miss Cecile.

"Heyyy, if it isn't my favorite nurse!"

Miss Cecile turned and spotted him, and a wide smile slid over her face. "I declare, it's Tyler Collens!"

"The one and only." He chuckled, stooping to kiss her dusky cheek.

"'Bout time you showed your face around here." She swatted his arm playfully.

"Hey, I'm here all the time. It's you who doesn't work in the ED anymore."

She smiled and shrugged. "Fair enough. It is good to see your pretty face again," she said, reaching up to pat his cheek.

He grinned. Long ago, he'd adopted Miss Cecile as a second mom. "Yours too. Unfortunately, I can't stay long, as I have to get back to Murrae. But I'm looking for someone, and I hoped you could help me."

Miss Cecile's eyebrows shot up and she planted her hands on her wide hips. "Well, now, it's about darn time you finally settled down—"

"Whoaaa." He raised his hands as stop signs. "Not that kind of looking for someone." Her face fell, and he had to laugh. "Sorry, you're going to have to find someone else to use your matchmaking skills on."

She shook her finger at him. "Oh, I will, boy. Don't you worry about that."

He shook his head, grinning again, then grew more serious. "Listen, Ezra and I brought in a little girl yesterday evening. I heard she was admitted, and I just wanted to see how she's doing."

Miss Cecile gave him a look and appeared to be thinking. "Well, you know I can't give you any info, but her mother is with her, so I'll ask her if you can pop in for sec."

Perfect. "Thanks, Miss Cecile. You're the best."

She waved a hand. "Ohh, you say that to anyone who'll do you a favor. Now come along."

Tyler followed her toward the pediatrics ward and stopped to knock on a door before entering. Within a minute, she stepped back out and motioned to him. He thanked her with another kiss on her cheek and entered the room, the door quietly clicking shut behind him. A worn, middle-aged woman seated next to the bed rose when she saw him, and he held out a hand. "Tyler Collens, ma'am."

"Meredith. Thank you so much." She seemed a bit teary-eyed as she met his, and then caught sight of the bruise on his forehead. She reached toward it and covered her mouth with her other hand, struggling to hold back her emotions. "I am so, so sorry."

He gripped her hand, giving it a gentle squeeze with a small smile that he hoped was reassuring. "Please, don't worry about it. I just wanted to see how Lilah was doing." He glanced toward the bed where the little girl slept.

The woman's face softened as she looked at her daughter as well, then retook her seat, motioning to another chair on his side of the bed. He sat.

"She's doing well, thanks to you. The doctor said she had two broken ribs that punctured her lung, but he said there wasn't any other internal damage."

He nodded. "I'm glad to hear it."

She was quiet for a moment as she watched her daughter. "I just . . . I never thought he would do this. I should have left long ago." She choked on a sob and shook her head.

Tyler's heart ached for the family torn apart. He paused to consider a response. "I'm sure you did the best you could. And now you have a fresh start," he said softly.

She nodded, drawing a deep breath and straightening, palming away the tears. "Yes. A fresh start." Her glossy, espresso-colored eyes shifted to him again. "Thanks in part to you."

He dipped his head, feeling uncomfortable. "I was just glad to get Lilah the help she needed."

At her name, the little girl stirred, the sleep clouding her beautiful eyes slowly clearing away. When she noticed him, she started and drew back. He watched the fear he'd seen the other night fill her eyes again, causing his chest to clench. He didn't want to be a cause of fear to this little girl who already feared too much.

But suddenly she relaxed and her eyes brightened, as if she recognized him. Then her lips tilted up in a teeny-tiny, shy smile.

Tyler smiled back, the ache in his chest lessening. Leaning forward slightly, his shoulders hunched in a non-threatening posture, he rested his forearms on his thighs. "Hi, Lilah."

Her finger twisted the corner of the white sheet as she stared at him. Then, softly, "Hi."

Meredith looked from him to her daughter, seeming surprised—maybe that she had responded at all. Gripping her daughter's other hand, she said, "Lilah, this is Mr. Tyler. Do you remember him?"

Lilah nodded.

"You know, Lilah, I have a daughter, and she's almost two years old." He held up two fingers. "She loves dollies. Do you like dollies too?"

She nodded again, soberly.

Tyler reached into his pocket and pulled out three small items that fit into the palm of his hand. "I thought so. See, I found these, and my daughter already has lots of dollies. I thought maybe you would like them. Maybe they can keep you company while you're staying here. What do you think?" He held out his hand, palm up, and Lilah tilted her head and carefully inspected the three items—three colorful pocket dolls. She looked up at her mom, and Meredith nodded, a smile on her face.

The little girl reached out and picked them up one at a time, a smile slowly growing on her face as she held them. She looked up at her mother again.

"What do you say, Li?" she asked.

Lilah looked at him. "Thank you, Mr. Tyler."

He couldn't help the grin. "Thank *you* for giving them a good home. I know you'll keep them safe. They couldn't live in my pocket forever."

A tiny giggle escaped her, and his heart soared at the sweet sound.

"They don't have names yet. Do you think you can name them too?"

Over the next ten minutes, Lilah thoughtfully named each of the dollies, and as Tyler watched, a sparkle grew in her too-grown-up eyes until she looked like the little girl that she was again. It made him want to grin, and he suddenly knew why he'd felt the need to come. Bringing a little bit of joy to this tiny soul was more than enough reward for the trip.

Finally, he pushed to his feet, saying he needed to go pick up his daughter. Lilah asked him to say hi to Murrae, and he agreed with a smile. Then she grew suddenly shy and leaned over to whisper something to her mother. Meredith looked up at him.

"Lilah wants to know if she can give you a hug," she said softly.

He smiled down at Lilah. "Of course you can give me a hug." He bent down and gently wrapped an arm around her small shoulders, her arms twining around his neck. He held her carefully, cautious of her ribs. She held on for a few moments before she let go and said, "Bye, Mr. Tyler."

He chucked her under her chin gently and smiled. "Bye, Lilah. Feel better soon, all right?"

She nodded with another smile. Tyler looked at Meredith, who motioned to the door. He stepped out and waited as she closed the door behind them and turned to him. She looked up at him and started to say something, but her face crumpled and she broke into tears, hands covering her face.

Suddenly uncomfortable, Tyler shifted on his feet. "Hey, what's wrong?" He wrapped an arm around her shoulders in a loose hug as she continued crying. After a few moments, the torrent seemed to stop, and she stepped back, wiping her face.

Taking a deep breath, she looked up at him. "You have no idea what this meant to Lilah. To me. My girls have never had a man treat them the way you treated Lilah." Her voice faltered. "Thank you."

He gripped her hand gently. "It was my pleasure. Honestly. Lilah's a sweetheart."

She nodded, wiping her eyes again. "Thank you. Your wife and daughter are very blessed."

His jaw tightened, but he managed a small smile. "Thank you, but . . . my wife died shortly after Murrae's birth."

Meredith considered him for a moment. "You've seen your share of pain too. And yet you're still so kind. God bless you." She pulled him into a hug.

He patted her back. "God bless you, too, Meredith. I'll be praying for you and your daughters."

She smiled. "Thank you, Tyler."

He gave a nod, then started down the corridor. He blew out a deep breath, his chest weighted with emotion, but he felt more fulfilled than he had in a long while.

That was an hour not wasted.

Chapter Ten

"Piper said she's going to put together a grand reopening party once everything is finished here," Alyvia commented after a few moments of silence as she and Tyler worked. He'd been over faithfully a few nights a week for the past two weeks, wielding screwdrivers and hammers, vacuum cleaners and jokes.

It was Tuesday night, and they were finishing some of the indoor things before a whole crew of people arrived Friday morning to fix the roof.

Her dream was finally coming true.

"A party? That's awesome." The screech of the drill punctuated his sentence as he worked on installing a new row of bookshelves.

Alyvia ran the iron across a curtain panel that was destined for the front windows, then leaned her elbows on the ironing board. "Tyler . . . Can I ask you a question?"

He glanced over his shoulder at her with a grin. "Sure, but that question doesn't guarantee you an answer, you realize."

She chuckled. "Fair enough. I . . . I wondered—"

"Mommommommommom!" Murrae's vigorous yell from her playpen caught both of their attention, and they laughed.

"One second, 'Rae. Daddy's busy," Tyler said as he inserted the last screw into the bookshelf.

"No! Want Mom!" The little girl reached her arms toward Alyvia.

She froze and her eyes darted toward Tyler. He turned around to see what had happened. Shock washed across his face, mixed with something else. Something painful to see.

Grief.

She tore her eyes from his stunned expression and stepped to pick up Murrae. "Not Mom, silly girl," she said in a forced lighthearted tone. "I'm Lyv."

The girl giggled and patted her cheeks with her tiny, pudgy hands. "Mom Lyv."

Alyvia's heart clenched. Murrae was just a little girl that didn't know better, but she couldn't imagine how Tyler felt. She glanced over her shoulder at him, but he'd disappeared behind the bookshelf, and she heard the sound of tools clanking together.

"C'mon, sweetie, let's go find a book." Alyvia went to the children's section, thinking to give Tyler a few minutes. Five minutes later, after she finished a second book, Tyler gingerly sank onto one of the kiddie size chairs.

"Wow, are these the wrong size."

She laughed. She laughed a lot when Tyler was around. That was part of the reason why she liked his company. "You think? All done for the night?"

"Yep." He nodded. "I used so many screws, those bookshelves aren't going anywhere for at least a decade."

Alyvia smiled, glad he seemed to have recovered from earlier. "Time to go home, sweetie," she said as she stood Murrae up from her lap.

The little girl went to her daddy and he sat her on his lap. "Not so fast. You had a question for me," he said, referring to their earlier conversation.

Snap. She didn't want to bring it up now. "Um, well, it's not important. It can wait."

"No, go ahead. You have my full attention," he said with a grin. Leaning forward, the chair creaked, and he winced.

She bit her lip, hesitating. "I just . . . I just wondered how . . . what . . . happened to Murrae's mom? It's not really any of my business, I know. And I don't want to pry. I am just curious, I guess. You don't have to answer if you don't want to," she finished in a rush.

Tyler leaned back in the chair—its creak again protesting his weight—and took a deep breath, the grin gone from his face now. "Oh."

Alyvia fiddled with a snag on her jeans. "Like I said, you don't have to answer."

"No, it's . . . it's okay." He paused, looking down at his daughter. "Cancer," he said simply after a long moment. "It all happened so fast. We found out she was pregnant with this munchkin—" a smile tinged his lips as he kissed her head. "Then, just a couple of months later, after some routine blood tests for her pregnancy . . . We got the diagnosis." He shook his head with an empty chuckle. "Worst day of my life. From the start, Sabrina handled it better than I did. She was a rockstar through the whole thing." He smiled softly, clearly lost in the past. "I miss her so much, but it's been . . . less lately, you know? I think it will always be there, the missing her, but some days are worse than others. When Murrae . . ." He shook his head again. "I've never said the word 'mom' to her. I talk about Sabrina and show Murrae her picture, but it's always 'mama.' So when she said that . . ."

"I'm sorry, Ty. I didn't—"

"It's not your fault. She's clearly gotten attached to you, and that doesn't bother me." He smiled at her. "You're a nice person to know."

She smiled faintly. "You don't have to answer this either, but . . . Do you think you'll ever remarry?"

His eyes met hers—icy blue, but not cold. Strange. "Yes," he said simply. "Someday. To the right person."

She felt as if there was some hidden meaning to his words, but she was too afraid to think hard enough to figure it out. Finally, he broke eye contact, shifting in the chair and pulling out his wallet from his back pocket. He flipped it open and drew out a small, tattered photograph.

Murrae's sleepy eyes brightened when she saw it. "Mama!" she said while pointing to the picture. Tyler grinned, and Alyvia felt her heart both melting and breaking. Melting at the adorable daddy-daughter duo, but breaking at the knowledge of what the small family had been through.

Tyler held out the image to Alyvia, and she grasped it carefully, instinctively recognizing the almost reverent way he handled it and feeling the need to treasure it. She flipped the tattered photo paper over and studied the photograph, inwardly giving a small gasp of surprise.

Sabrina Collens had long, dark, glossy brown hair and bright hazel eyes. The photo had been captured mid-laugh, and her expression was a pure joy that almost made whoever looked at it want to laugh along with her. A generous dose of freckles that scattered across her nose and cheeks only gave her beautiful face more character. In a word, she was stunning.

She smiled up at Tyler and handed it back. "She was beautiful. And Murrae looks just like her."

He nodded and thoughtfully tucked it back into his wallet before gazing down at his daughter. "Yeah. Her eyes are all she got from me, thank goodness," he said with a laugh, running a knuckle down Murrae's cheek. After a pause, he shifted. "Well, we better get home." He hefted Murrae in his arms and pushed to his feet. "Goodnight."

"Goodnight, Tyler," she said softly as she watched him stride to the front of the store, grab Murrae's backpack and throw it over his shoulder, and leave, the bell on the door tinkling as it closed behind him.

What astonished her about Tyler Collens was that he'd been through so much but hadn't let it affect his indomitable and infectious joy.

She set aside the books on her lap and stood, crossing her arms. She couldn't help but admire that about him.

Chapter Eleven

Tyler laid Murrae in her crib and leaned a hip against the rail, watching her sigh and shift in her sleep.

She'd called Alyvia "mom."

He hadn't been prepared, and the moment had felt like a dagger. He liked Alyvia. But Sabrina was Murrae's mom. And he ached in a completely different way, knowing that the little girl would never know her true mother.

His thumb rubbed the smoothed skin of his fourth finger where his wedding band had resided for just over two years of marriage. He had taken it off just a few months ago, symbolizing a time to move on. But that hadn't lessened his love for her or his commitment to have and to hold until death parted them.

He'd never anticipated as he said those words and slipped the ring on her finger that the parting would come so soon.

He turned and quietly pulled the door shut and automatically walked to the piano keyboard sitting in the corner of the already-small living area. Sinking onto the bench with a sigh, his fingers found their place of their own accord, and a simple, soft, sad melody sounded out. Closing his eyes, he let his fingers pour out the notes he couldn't put into words, the melody rising as a prayer.

After several minutes, it crescendoed, his long fingers stretching to octaves in the left hand. It continued that way, the deeper tones of the lower keys almost discordant at times, wrestling, fighting for dominance.

And then they stilled, as if a hush washed over them, and the melody wound down to a single, final note.

His hands dropped from the keys to his lap as his head bowed and his chest heaved with emotion.

Tetelestai.

The Greek word that meant *It is finished* floated into his head, bringing a calm to his mind along with a hint of grief.

Endings could be both joy-filled and grief-filled.

Endings were bittersweet.

It's time to move on. To live again.

Chapter Twelve

"This oughta be the last bolt," Tyler said. He lay on his back, head stuck under the sink in the small bookstore bathroom.

"Do you even have any idea what you're doing?" Alyvia asked, arms crossed, standing a few steps away, surveying his work. Tyler insisted she was hovering.

"Nope." A crash, then he sucked in a sharp breath. "Jiminy Cricket," came his mutter.

"Are you okay?" she asked, crouching down, but still unable to see his face.

"Nope, might die."

She paused and frowned. He was joking, clearly. But . . . "So are you okay?"

He scooted out from beneath the sink, a grin on his face. "I'm fine, Lyv, thanks for asking. Just dropped the wrench and scraped my knuckles a bit." He displayed a fist, the knuckles of his third and fourth fingers scraped and oozing blood.

"Oh. Ouch."

"That's it? 'Oh ouch'?" Tyler affected a wounded look.

"What, did you want me to get you a Dora the Explorer band-aid and kiss your boo-boo?"

He smirked. "I prefer Diego."

Alyvia widened her eyes in shock. "Prefer? As in, present tense?"

He looked confused for a moment, then shifted. "Hey, I have an almost-two-year-old."

"Uh-huh."

"Stop picking on a wounded man." Tyler slid back under the sink, and a couple seconds later he called out, "Alrighty, turn 'er on."

"Got it." She hopped up and turned the knob on the sink slowly at first, then all the way, watching as the water eased from a trickle to a downpour.

Suddenly, Tyler yelled. "Turn it off! Hurry up!"

She quickly did so, then watched as he slid back out and sat up. She stared at him for a moment, then a giggle slipped out. She tried not to let it, but it did anyway.

Tyler just stared at her as he swiped water from his eyes, his blond hair matted to his head and dripping droplets onto the tile floor.

She covered her mouth with her hand, trapping the mirth trying to escape. "Wha . . . What happened?"

"Leak in the pipe," he said dryly.

Alyvia snorted. "I'll . . . go grab a towel." She hurried to grab one from the back room, still giggling, and handed it to him. He took it and scrubbed it vigorously over his head, sending droplets flying.

Finally, he chuckled and shook his head. "Well then."

She couldn't help it any longer, and burst into laughter. Maybe it had been a long day. Or maybe it was his hair sticking up every which way from the towel drying as well as the chagrined look on his face. Or maybe it was because the whole situation was absurd—the two of them crammed into the tiny bathroom, him on the floor, wet, and with his long legs bent to be able to fit. Tyler glanced up at her as she shook with laughter, and he chuckled too. Soon they were both belly-laughing.

And it felt really good. Him. Her. Laughing. Together.

It scared her how natural it felt to be herself around him. It was comfortable, easy-going.

And terrifying.

Tyler took a deep breath, an ache in his side from laughing so hard. He couldn't put his finger on what was different, but something was.

Maybe it was the elephant that was no longer sitting on his chest.

"Somebody better clean up this mess," he said as their laughter wound down. He placed his fingertips in a puddle of water on the floor and flicked the droplets at Alyvia. She squealed and backed away. "I nominate you, since it was your fault," he said, flicking water at her again.

"Stop it!" She held her hands up in front of her face, but giggled. It was a cute sound. "And what makes this my fault?"

"You turned the water on."

She laughed. "Ohh, no, you don't, sir! I'm not the one who 'fixed' the sink." She used finger quotes on the word.

He laughed again and flicked more water, causing her to squeal and go running. "Hey, wait! At least help me up. I think my legs are permanently bent in this position."

"Help yourself up. You're a big boy," she called back as a cell phone rang.

"Exactly my point," he muttered with a grunt as he pulled himself off the floor, waiting a moment until the cramp in his right leg loosened. His body was not meant for small spaces and hard floors. He heard her answer her phone with a cheery "This is Alyvia," as he pulled his shirt off and wrung the water out of a portion of it before pulling it back over his head. He couldn't help but overhear the one-sided conversation as he ambled back to the front of the store.

"Uh, hi. How's it going?" Her casual tone turned guarded and he wondered at the change as he leaned against the front counter and pulled his own phone out of his pocket to check his messages.

"Um, well . . . I . . ." Tyler glanced up and saw that her face was screwed up in a wince before she sent him a pleading glance. "I have plans tonight."

Tyler's brows rose, and the look he gave her conveyed silent question marks.

"Sorry. Yeah, of course. Sure. Bye." Alyvia hung up and dropped the phone on the counter with a loud sigh before dropping into the office chair herself.

Tyler waited a moment. "What was all that about?"

She looked over at him, that unmistakable pleading look back on her face. "Do you have plans tonight?"

"No?" He drew the word out in a question.

"Well . . ." Alyvia leaned her elbows on the desk and appeared to be texting. After a moment, she set her phone down and looked up at him with a smile. "Now we wait."

He chuckled. "For?"

Her smile turned mischievous. "We just wait. Now, I'll go get Murrae; you go clean up the water in the bathroom," she said as Murrae let out a whine from where she had been contentedly playing in her playpen.

"Hey, that's not fair," he protested as she grabbed a mop from the supply closet and tossed it to him. He caught it before the wood handle smacked his head.

She laughed as she picked up Murrae and pressed a kiss to her cheek, seemingly without even giving it a thought. "As far as my soggy memory recalls, you were the one 'fixing' my bathroom. So it seems perfectly fair to me. Don'tcha think so, Murrae?"

Murrae grinned at him, not having a clue about anything. "Tink so."

Tyler laughed. "All right, fine. Murrae has spoken." He held the mop aloft as he headed back toward the bathroom. After mopping up the water and tidying up his tools, he took note of the pipe under the sink that would need to be replaced—he'd hit the hardware store tomorrow. He placed the mop back on its hook in the closet and looked for Alyvia. He found her sitting cross-legged on the floor behind the front desk, texting, and Murrae kneeling in front of her, sipping on the turquoise water bottle he was ninety-nine percent sure belonged to Alyvia.

Alyvia looked up at his footsteps and gave a look of dismay when she saw Murrae with her water bottle. Tyler chuckled. "Sorry, she's obsessed with water bottles. I can't keep mine from her. You'll want to wash it before you use it again."

She giggled. "I see that." She extricated the bottle from the little girl's clasp, set it aside, and pulled Murrae into her lap before looking up at him. "So. You don't have plans tonight . . . How about a picnic in the park?"

His heart stuttered in surprise. Was she . . . asking him on a . . . he almost didn't dare think the word . . . a date? He coughed in an attempt to hide the shock. "What?"

She grinned and hugged Murrae closer. "Oh, and we'd be babysitting, too. Ezra and Piper are going to see a movie, so we'd be watching the kids. If you don't object, that is."

Tyler felt the arrhythmia even out. *Oh.* "Does this have anything to do with your phone call?"

She winced. "I said I had plans, which was a tiny white lie, but technically, I was already considering plans, so . . . it wasn't completely untrue."

He nodded with a shrug. "Okay. Well, I don't mind babysitting if you don't. Piper and Ezra could probably use some alone time anyway."

She smiled. "That's what I thought."

Chapter Thirteen

Alyvia cuddled three-month-old Haevyn close to her chest and watched as Tyler went back and forth taking turns pushing Topher and Murrae on adjacent swings. Both children giggled gleefully and Topher screamed "Higher!" with each push.

But Alyvia found herself watching Tyler. His blond hair, slightly too long, blew in the breeze, and she noticed his eyes crinkled up as he laughed at the kids' joy. It was an adorable sight—a massive, six-four dude playing with little ones. It brought a smile to her own face.

She laughed as Topher gave a screech of delight at his newfound heights and cupped a hand around her mouth. "Careful, Ty, I don't want to see the pizza they ate again," she called.

Tyler looked her way and laughed, gradually letting the swings slow—much to the little boy's chagrin. She watched as he picked Murrae up out of the swing-chair and settled her on his hip before helping Topher slide to the ground—where he promptly took off like a shot toward the mini climbing wall.

This was much better than having to do dinner with her dad. She wasn't ready for that yet. The thought of sitting in a restaurant, just the two of them, having to fill conversation for an hour or more was exhausting in and of itself.

What did one say to the father who committed from the start to be there for his family, then wasn't? To the man who broke promises and hearts when he walked out the door without looking back? To the dad who thought he could just waltz back into lives as if he hadn't left devastation in his wake ten years ago when he left?

Yeah. She didn't think she could handle that any time soon, and while her conscience still niggled at her white-lie excuse, she couldn't help but feel relieved to be *here* instead of *there*.

Shaking his head, Tyler walked toward her. "The boundless energy of that boy is insane."

Alyvia chuckled and bounced Haevyn slightly as she squirmed. "Makes me wonder how his mom does it."

"Makes me wonder how *my* mom did it," Tyler said with a small laugh, again shaking his head.

She turned more toward him and squinted at him with a half-smile. "You were pretty crazy as a kid too, huh? I can see that."

"Ohh, wow, I can't tell if that was a compliment or not. But yes, I was a bit 'cray-cray.'" He used finger quotes.

Alyvia laughed to hear a grown man use that slang term. "A bit?"

"Okay, so I broke a collarbone, a wrist, and had dislocated my shoulder all before age ten," he admitted ruefully.

"What?" she gave a shocked laugh. "Tell me not all at the same time, right?"

"Thankfully, no. The collarbone was when I was six, and my sister dared me to climb a tree; the wrist was a fall off my bike at seven; and the dislocated shoulder was a fall off the shed roof at ten. Got in big trouble for that one."

"I'll bet. Were you grounded for a month?"

"Just about. I had to promise to keep both feet strictly on the ground for a whole six weeks." He shook his head and gave her a look. "For a ten-year-old, that's a long time to not climb trees, walk fences, or play on playgrounds."

She smothered a chuckle. "Yikes."

He laughed. "Yeah." Murrae scrambled to get down, so he set her on the ground and they both watched as she hurried toward where Topher was pushing around the empty tire swing. "So what about you? Were you a wild child, or not so much?"

She smirked at him. "What do you think?"

He offered the pretense of giving it some thought. "Hmm. I'd say you were more the bookish sort who liked reading and schoolwork on rainy days. But then you have three brothers, so I'm sure you helped build your fair share of forts over the years."

She gaped at him for a moment, and it was his turn to smirk.

"Pretty accurate, huh?"

She recovered herself and laughed. He'd pegged her. "Actually, yes. My brothers were always dragging me around for football games and building forts. Although I guess I tagged along and begged to be a part as much as they dragged." She smiled fondly, remembering. She'd loved those times. Before things got complicated.

"Were you and your siblings close?" he asked.

"Very. We still are. We've become a bit scattered, especially with Maddison in Seattle, but we're still as close as we can be."

Just then, a wail sounded and they both turned toward the sound. It looked as if the tire swing had hit Murrae and knocked her onto her backside, where she sat sobbing in the wood chips. Topher was nearly crying himself in sympathy as he squatted next to her. In the split second, she saw panic light Tyler's eyes as he rushed toward them. Alyvia wasn't far behind. She watched as Tyler dropped to his knees beside his daughter, scooping her up in his arms and looking her over. Alyvia knelt as well and pulled Topher to her side and comforted him. "Is she okay?"

Tyler pulled a white handkerchief out of his jeans pockets—who still carried handkerchiefs?—and dabbed at the blood seeping from Murrae's lip. The little girl still screamed. Tyler nodded and took a deep breath. "Just a split lip, looks like."

"Aw, poor honey. It's okay, Topher. 'Rae's all right. She just has an owie."

Topher sniffled. "Owie?"

Tyler gently brushed the tears from Murrae's cheeks and shushed her softly before pushing to his feet and cuddling her on his shoulder. The sobs slowly eased to sniffles as he patted her back.

Alyvia stood too, bouncing a now wide-awake baby. Tyler's face was tucked against Murrae, so she took advantage of that to watch him curiously. His shoulders were rigid and he seemed incredibly tense for such a seemingly small issue. Didn't little children get owies all the time? She wouldn't have pegged him for a helicopter parent, but . . .

Tyler looked up as Murrae quieted, looking subdued himself. "We should probably go."

She nodded. "Come on, bud, it's time to go home," she addressed Topher.

The little boy started to whine but quickly stopped at Tyler's sharp command to obey. It wasn't harsh, but she'd never heard him address someone, let alone a child, like that. She eyed him warily as they headed toward their cars. They'd driven separately, as car seats for all three children wouldn't have fit in one of their cars. They quickly buckled the three tired children in.

"See you at Ezra's house," Tyler called as he opened his truck door.

"Ty, wait." Alyvia leaned over the roof of her small car to look at him. "Are you all right?" she asked softly.

His brow rippled as he paused. "I'm fine."

"You seem upset."

He shrugged, looking out over the playground before looking back at her. "Murrae got hurt. It could have been a lot worse."

"But, she's fine." Her words came out hesitantly as she tried to read his angst.

"Yeah." He smiled weakly.

Tyler climbed into his truck, slammed the door, and cranked the engine, waiting until Alyvia pulled out before following. He glanced into the rearview mirror at Murrae before turning out of the parking lot and onto the street. She was looking out the window, eyes drooping in tiredness. Her bottom lip was slightly swollen, although not badly, and the bleeding had stopped. Blowing out a breath through pursed lips, he adjusted his grip on the wheel and scrubbed a hand across his mouth.

He'd overreacted to a tiny incident. In front of Alyvia. And she'd picked up on it.

Aw, shoot.

Never would he have pegged himself as the over-protective, over-worried helicopter dad. But he was doing a darn good job of it, and he had no idea why.

Maybe because he already nearly lost Murrae—a couple of times in the beginning. Maybe because he'd lost Sabrina.

His fingers ruined his combed hair, then rubbed across his mouth again. So maybe he did know.

He needed to chill.

But his gut was still in a knot at the thought of something worse than a busted lip happening to his dark-haired little angel in the back seat—his whole world.

God, it's harder than I imagined, being a dad. Not to mention doing it alone. I don't want to be afraid.

His mind put a mental finger on the word he didn't know he was looking for.

He was afraid.

Who said anything about doing it alone? The voice floated into his consciousness and he almost had to chuckle.

Got me there, God.

He turned into Piper and Ezra's driveway behind Alyvia and pulled the keys out. In a shorter time than he thought possible, they got all three kids out of the cars, washed up, and in PJs. He settled on the couch with a bottle for Haevyn. Murrae snuggled up under his opposite arm while Alyvia settled Topher in bed and read him a story to wind down the somehow still feisty little guy.

After a while, Alyvia finally stepped out of the bedroom and quietly shut the door, a look of relief on her face as she sank into the recliner across from him. "Goodness. He was a bit wound up."

Tyler chuckled softly. "I think he's always like that."

"You're probably right." Her half-smile had a touch of exasperation.

A few beats of silence passed. Alyvia yawned, causing Tyler to smother a yawn as he set aside the bottle and shifted the baby upright to pat her back. "So, you gonna tell me what that phone call earlier was about?"

She wrinkled her nose, eliciting a dimple in her left cheek. She fiddled with a snag on her dark wash jeans before looking up again, but her eyes drifted past his head. "My dad wanted to do dinner tonight."

He waited for her to continue, his rhythmic pats the only sound. He guessed Murrae had conked out at his elbow.

"He and I don't have the best of relationships . . . So, things are just . . . awkward, I guess. He left when I was fifteen. I never really knew why. There was just . . . a lot of tension all the time, ya know?" She met his eyes for the first time since starting, and he nodded. "Anyway, I've only seen him occasionally over the last—" her nose wrinkled again as she thought "—ten years or so. But he moved back to Arlington a couple of months ago, and . . . I don't know what he wants. It's like he wants to be a part of the family again."

"And you're not sure how you feel about that."

She shook her head with that rueful smile again. "I just don't believe it's as simple as he thinks."

"I can understand that."

There was an awkward silence as he tried to think of something else to say, but he came up with nothing.

Alyvia waved a hand and sighed. "Sorry, I didn't mean to unload that on you."

"That's okay. People say I'm a good listener." He paused. "Actually, no one says that."

She laughed, as he'd been hoping she would. The subject changed, and they spent a few more minutes chatting about random things before he realized it was getting late—and he now had two sleeping little girls on him. Alyvia took Haevyn off his chest, and they said goodnight before she headed to the master bedroom to lay her in her bassinet. Tyler picked up a limp Murrae and quickly had her buckled in her car seat and cozied in a soft blanket. She was still sound asleep.

As he drove through the quiet, dark city streets, lit intermittently by streetlights, he found himself feeling strangely content. He'd enjoyed the evening, despite the tense moments. He liked hanging out with the kids. And he was finding he very much liked hanging out with Alyvia.

But he forced himself not to dwell on that thought.

Chapter Fourteen

A lyvia woke up on Saturday morning and promptly rolled out of bed. Usually, it took a bit to get herself functional and on her feet when she woke up, but when she had plans for the day, she was better at getting up quicker. And she planned to get her apartment in order today.

The apartment above the bookstore was small, but roomy enough for a single resident. There was a small main area that served as kitchen, dining room, and living room. A tiny bathroom with barely enough room for a shower was off to the left when you came up the stairs, and just past that was her small bedroom. Anything larger than a twin bed wouldn't have fit in the tight space. As it was, she managed to work in a small dresser next to the closet, and she planned to hang a large mirror above it—those interior decorators on HGTV said it made the room look bigger. Getting a nightstand and a hanging bookshelf would give it the homey touch it lacked.

As of now, boxes still cluttered the floors, yet to be unpacked, and she wanted to get the main area painted before she settled in any further. That nasty oak wainscotting straight from the '90s needed to go. She thought painting the walls a nice bright white would make things a little classier.

In her head, she went over her mental to-do list for the day as she brushed her teeth, took a shower, and dried her hair. Finished dressing, she checked the time. Nearly nine a.m. She started. *Sheesh, time is moving too fast for this early in the morning.*

The morning flew by in like manner as she cleaned, organized, and prepped the walls for painting, all while greeting and checking out the intermittent customers that came through the doors. She now knew why people had bells on doors—but her legs were starting to ache from constantly running up and down the stairs.

It was nearly noon before she stopped for a breath and the hollow feeling in her stomach shouted that she'd never eaten breakfast. She had, however, downed three cups of coffee throughout the morning. Thankfully, it was half-decaf coffee, otherwise she probably would have passed out from the caffeine rush. But she loved coffee way too much to do away with it entirely, so half-decaf it was.

As she was contemplating what her refrigerator might hold for lunch, the bell rang from downstairs. Blowing out a breath, she found herself hoping it would be Tyler—then chided herself for the thought. He had a life. She grabbed her water bottle and gulped twice before clattering down the stairs, stopping before entering the main area of the store to brush back the wispy pieces of her ponytail that had escaped. Stepping around bookshelves to reach the front desk, she settled in her chair and searched for her customer. She spotted a man standing at the new releases shelf, his back to her and head bent as he looked at a book. Tall, with nearly black hair that was tinging toward gray, there was something familiar in the way he stood.

She cleared her throat and put on a smile. "Good morning! Or, goodness, almost afternoon. Can I help you find something, or are you just browsing?"

The man turned toward her at her cheery words, and despite the lines on his face as he smiled and shoulders that stooped more than they had, she had no trouble recognizing him. Her smile slowly faded in her shock.

"Hey, Alyvia." His voice seemed stilted, like he was trying very hard to be casual. He glanced around and waved a hand. "Your mom keeps talking about what a great job you're doing with this place, so I figured it was about time I took a look for myself."

There was silence for a few seconds, and her brain screamed, *Speak*! Her pulse throbbed in her temple and she had to swallow twice before she found her voice. "Dad. Uh, hi." She clasped her hands together and rested them on the desk to steady them.

He's here. Here. In my bookstore. Three months of successfully avoiding a face-to-face encounter—okay, so she'd admit that that was her goal, even if it had been an unconscious one at the time—and now he was here. He'd sought her out.

And Mom had blabbed.

She gulped again and tried to find her bearings. *Now what?* "Uh, how've you been?" she asked, then mentally facepalmed. But then, was there a guidebook for What to Say to Your Dad When You Haven't Seen Him in Years? If there was, she probably should have bought it. She would have stocked copies.

"Doing all right, thanks." He set the book back on its shelf and turned more fully to face her. But he didn't step any closer to the desk, as if he knew she might run like a scared rabbit if he did. His voice and eyes—the same depthless green she remembered—softened. "How are you, Lyvy?"

She couldn't control the small flinch at the nickname only he had ever used. It felt like a blow, a knife just below the ribs. "I . . ." She rallied and mustered a smile. "I'm doing good. Do you want a tour?" She came around the desk, wanting to do anything but, but even she was above completely dissing someone.

At least, in person.

"Sure, that'd be great," he said, following her.

Using the cheery, friendly voice she used when speaking with all her customers—while praising herself for her control—she gave him a tour of each section of the store. From the non-fiction, to the myriad fiction categories, to the colorful children's section, to the cute little coffee corner she was so proud of. She even pointed out the tiny bathroom that was looking—and functioning—quite nicely, thanks to Tyler's elbow grease. As she looked at her space through someone else's eyes, she found herself proud of the culmination of her hard work. This had been her dream for so long, and now it was finally coming true. She wondered what her father thought—then wished she didn't. She didn't need his approval, acceptance, or love.

But a piece of her heart ached for it nonetheless. The same part of her heart that at six, nine, thirteen, and then fifteen years old had tried so hard to please her moody and even surly father. The part of her heart that so badly wanted to see him smile over something she had accomplished. She didn't need a "good job" or a pat on the back. She just wanted to see a smile light his face and know she had put it there.

And then that fifteen-year-old's heart had broken under the weight of striving, and she realized that no amount of trying would please him, and so she'd stopped. Stopped trying. Stopped caring.

Alyvia blew out a quiet breath and shook off the thoughts. She turned to face him, forcing a smile into place and clasping her hands together. "Well, that's pretty much it. Except for the back room and the upstairs apartment. I just moved in last weekend, but I'm sure Mom mentioned that too." Among other things.

Her dad's head nodded and he tucked his hands into the pockets of his khakis. He smiled and spoke softly, almost shyly. "It looks good, Lyvy. Real good." He cleared his throat, as if the words were unfamiliar and had tickled on the way out.

Alyvia's shoulders eased a fraction, the unconscious tension lessening. She gave a short nod, then the bell at the front of the store rang, breaking the silence and saving her from the awkwardness. "Duty calls," she said with a small smile, turning away and hurrying toward the front desk. *Hurrying to help the customer, not hurrying away from Dad.*

As she chatted with the customer, helped them find a set of books, rang up the purchase, and said goodbye, her mind spun, wondering where her father was and what he was doing. Half of her hoped he had left without her noticing, but that wasn't likely. Finally, she looked up and caught sight of him heading toward her, book in hand. He set the 1700s historical fiction novel on the counter and nudged it to her.

"Never can leave a bookstore without buying a book," he said with a wry smile, the sight almost unfamiliar.

"It's like walking into a restaurant and not eating," she muttered by rote but trailed off as she realized what she'd said.

She sometimes forgot she'd inherited her love of books from her father. She always remembered him happiest when he was reading, in a bookstore, or talking about books. Books equaled happiness when it came to her father, and so while she'd at first started reading some children's classics just to be able to discuss them with him, she had soon come to love them as much as he did.

She quickly rang up his book and wrapped it in brown paper printed with whimsical stars, glancing up once to find him watching her, studying her. Finished, she pushed it back across the counter toward him, swiped his credit card, and then placed the receipt and card on top of the book. He thanked her, pocketing them and picking up the book. He turned toward the door, then paused, angling back to face her. He cleared his throat. "Hey, maybe we could grab dinner sometime soon? Catch up a bit. I'd like to . . . to talk." He peered at her, and the insecurity in his gaze and posture crumbled some of her walls.

She nodded and managed a non-committal, "Sure."

He gave a slow nod back and turned again, this time making it out the door. From her place behind the counter, she watched until he disappeared down the sidewalk. Was it just her imagination, or were his shoulders more stooped than they had been when he'd walked in?

Perhaps for the first time, she saw a glimpse past her own fear and pain and bitterness. And saw a broken man. A broken man who was . . . trying.

Her fingers twisted knots in her hair. *God, I . . . I don't want to forgive him.*

But strangely enough, she found a tiny, little, itty-bitty piece of her actually *did*.

Chapter Fifteen

"Listen, munchkin," Tyler growled playfully, but a touch of frustration filtered through nonetheless as he tried to put a diaper on the squirming girl. Murrae was a bundle of tears and whines this morning, probably due to too much romping with Topher yesterday. The energy of the little boy was boundless, and Murrae did her best to keep up. This wouldn't be the first time the toddler had made them late for church, and he knew it wouldn't be the last. But he was frustrated anyway, because heaven help him, he was exhausted too. Half the night had been riddled with one of those restless, ongoing dreams you couldn't shake no matter how many times you woke up. The kind that wasn't quite a nightmare but was nonetheless disturbing.

His subconscious had been playing tricks with his mind. Sabrina was running away and he couldn't catch her. Then Murrae was with her, and they were too far away to hear him calling. He sobbed and fell to his knees as their images faded, and it was his own shout that woke him for the final time at five a.m.

He shook the memory of the dream from his head as he tugged a too-small dress over his daughter's head. His tiny preemie baby was growing like a weed. Maybe a trip to Target would be in order after church—assuming Murrae didn't crash and burn before then. She was getting an early nap today. He finished the buttons on her dress, then swiped a tissue from nearby to wipe the tears and snot from her face.

"There we go, 'Rae. Daddy's turn now." He kissed her round cheek and, after scooping her up in his arms, headed for his own room, where he deposited her on the bed. Nabbing a dark, blueish-green button-down shirt from a hanger in the closet, he pulled it on over the white t-shirt he wore and hurriedly buttoned it. He looked up and saw Murrae watching him with bright eyes and a paci in her mouth, her finger endlessly twisting a piece of hair. Her silky dark brown wisps were half curly and half snarled, but—he checked his watch as he buttoned his cuff—they were out of time to do anything about it. He tucked his shirt in, picked up Murrae, grabbed a box of her favorite crackers, and hurried out the door.

Fifteen minutes later, they walked into the small church building in the middle of one of the opening worship songs, and he sighed as he slid into a seat in the last row. He sat Murrae down at his feet with a toy and leaned back in the chair, closing his eyes and exhaling deeply. *All right, God. I'm here. I don't know why it has to be so darn hard just to find some time to spend in Your presence, but . . . I'm trying.*

Pushing all other thoughts from his mind with effort, he was able to focus on the speaker's encouraging sermon, only interrupted when Murrae got fussy during the ending prayer. He quickly scooped her up and stepped out of the room into the foyer, lightly patting her back until she dozed off as the service ended and people started leaving.

He caught sight of Ezra and Piper heading his way, their infant daughter in a wrap attached to Piper's chest, three-year-old Topher and a pink diaper bag in Ezra's arms. Tyler smiled. They made a cute little family. He knew the couple had been through their own set of troubles, but he still watched them approach somewhat bittersweetly, thinking they could have been him and Sabrina. He swallowed the lump rising in his throat and drummed up a smile.

"Heyyy, fam! Ezra, I have to say, I dig the pink purse," he threw out with a grin.

Ezra rolled his eyes. "It's a diaper bag, you nitwit. And hello to you too."

"Oh, is it? My bad." He winked at Piper, and she shook her head with a smile.

"Yes, and if I recall, you have one yourself, so you don't really have a leg to stand on," Ezra retorted.

"I assure you, I do not have a pink purse."

"Diaper bag."

Tyler ignored Ezra, lifting a hand to Topher for a high five. "Hey, little man. Whassup?"

The little boy pulled his finger out of his mouth and gave him a wet five. "'Aevyn threw up."

Tyler raised his eyebrows and nodded seriously at him. "Did she? Well, babies do that sometimes."

Topher nodded back at him just as seriously. "'Aevyn da baby. I'm big now."

Tyler chuckled and sized up the little boy. "Is that what your parents have been telling you?"

"Tyler!" Piper smacked his arm, and he laughed. Then he caught sight of Alyvia coming toward their group. He watched as she stopped to talk to someone, laughed, waved, then continued toward them.

"Earth to Tyler . . ." Ezra waved a hand in front of him, and Tyler started.

"What?"

His buddy glanced over his shoulder then leaned back on his heels to study him, a smirk slowly forming on his face.

Tyler frowned. "What's *that* look?"

"I think you know . . ." The smirk on Ezra's face was very irritating.

"It's not what you're thinking. Piper, hurry and change the subject. Ask me to dinner," he implored.

But she was grinning just as widely as she swayed slightly back and forth in the movement all mothers learned quickly. "I don't think I'm going to."

He groaned. "You two are cruel. Look, I'm going to— "

"Who's cruel?" Alyvia asked, finally reaching them.

Tyler sent Ezra a *don't you dare* look as Piper and Alyvia hugged. "Nobody's cruel. Piper and Ezra are great friends."

Ezra chuckled. "So, dinner, Tyler?"

"Sorry, no, actually. I have a grumpy child who will need another nap eventually, and said child also does not fit in any of her clothes, so we're making a Target trip."

"You're shopping for girls' clothes, Ty? Without me?" Piper looked laughingly incredulous.

"I know, I know. But I've got to sometime, and I figured when she's two would be easier than when she's twelve, right?"

Ezra groaned. "Let's not talk about shopping for clothes with twelve-year-old daughters. I don't even want to think about it."

Piper rolled her eyes and exchanged a look with Alyvia. "You two are pathetic. You've both got more than a decade before that happens, so stop freaking out."

Ezra pantomimed wiping his forehead, and Tyler chuckled.

"Speaking of daughters, this one needs to eat, so we better get going, Ez," Piper continued, working to shush her squirming little one.

"Alrighty, m'dear. Alyvia, that dinner invitation is, as always, extended to you as well."

She smiled gratefully. "Thanks, guys, but I think I'm going to pass this time."

"All right. See you later, you two."

"Sayonara." Tyler waved. The little family headed toward the exit, leaving the two of them—three counting the sleeping Murrae—alone.

Tyler was determined for this not to be awkward but had a feeling it might be. He fished for a topic of conversation, but Alyvia beat him to it.

She shifted around his shoulder to see Murrae, then said, "Shopping, huh?"

"Yep," he grimaced, then leaned in in a conspiratorial whisper. "I'm trying to prove to Piper— or probably more importantly, my mom—that I can successfully clothe my own daughter."

Alyvia giggled.

"Hey . . . want to save me from likely embarrassment and come with me? I think I could probably do it, but a female's opinion wouldn't be unwelcome. I can't say that Murrae has developed much in the way of opinions yet." He paused. "No, that's not true. She really doesn't like blueberries. In anything."

She smiled and ran her hand softly down the sleeping girl's curls. Tyler caught himself staring and shifted. "So how about it?"

Alyvia smiled up at him and his heart thudded a little faster. "Sure, why not?"

Chapter Sixteen

Alyvia undid the straps holding Murrae in her car seat and pulled the now-happy girl from her seat in the back of Tyler's truck. An excited "Lyv!" and other gibberish escaped the little girl, and Alyvia smiled, pressing a kiss to her squishy cheek. Murrae had her more than wrapped around those tiny fingers. She joined Tyler at the back of the truck and he tucked his phone in his pocket with a sigh and held out his arms.

"Want me to carry her?"

"No, I'm good. Is something wrong?" she asked.

"Huh? Oh, nah, not really." He tucked his hands in his pockets. "Just my mom. She wants me to come to Seattle to visit her and my dad," he said as they walked to the giant red entrance of the store.

"I didn't know you were from Seattle."

He cast a sidelong look at her. "Yep. Born and raised, but life as a paramedic in a big city can be harrowing, so I came here. Best decision I made, considering I found my lady love." A bittersweet grin slid onto his face before slowly fading.

"So, are you going to visit?" she asked, glancing up at him.

Shrugging, he pulled open the door for her to enter. "Probably. It's just a matter of when. It'd have to be over a weekend since I don't want to take time off work. I—" He paused and shook his head. "Sorry, I'm rambling. I think best out loud." He nudged her shoulder with his as she led the way to the children's section. "What about you? You from Arlington originally?"

"Born and raised." She tossed his words back at him with a grin. "Most of my siblings have scattered around the area—Aaron is still here; he's a doctor at Cascade Valley, and Micah's moving to be closer to his fiancée's family once they're married. Maddison is in Seattle, and Elliot's in Everett. Me, I've never been keen on leaving Arlington. I like it here. It's home."

Tyler stopped and stared at her with a chuckle. "Keen? Who uses words like that anymore?" he teased.

Alyvia rolled her eyes. "Me, obviously. Small town or not, some of us have more culture than others."

He laughed. "Touché." Then glanced around the store. "What are we here for again?"

"Very funny." She pointed to the little girls' section.

He followed the direction of her finger. "Oh, yeah." He rubbed the back of his neck. "That's a lot of pink."

She hid her smirk. "Oh, come now, surely you're man enough to handle it."

Straightening, he gave a cocky salute. "Challenge accepted, ma'am." Then he hesitated and pointed back the way they'd come. "I'm gonna go grab a cart."

Shaking her head at his antics, she turned toward a clothing rack. "Your dad's a silly man, isn't he?" she said to the little girl still in her arms.

Murrae craned her neck to look over Alyvia's shoulder. "Dada?"

"Yes, he'll be back in a minute." Alyvia checked the size of the dress the little girl was wearing, then started looking for clothes a size up. Tyler came back with a cart a few moments later and plopped Murrae in the seat of it, leaving Alyvia's arms free to search the racks.

"Your chariot, my princess," Tyler said as he buckled the little girl in, and Alyvia hid her smile in the clothing.

Tyler stopped the cart in front of a shelf of colorful pajamas and randomly chose two from the pile. He held them up in front of Murrae. "Which one, 'Rae?"

She tilted her head to the side as if considering, and Tyler chuckled. "Dat!" She pointed to the pink one on the left.

"'Dat' it is then, sunshine." He tossed it in the back of the cart and repeated the process. After several minutes, the little girl got restless and started to fight her way out of her seat.

"Okay, okay, so shopping isn't your thing either. Hopefully Lyv is having better luck than us," he said as he unbuckled her and put her on the ground. He took her hand and led her through the racks of clothing until he found Alyvia, her arm laden with clothing. He pulled them off her arm and dropped them in the cart. "Alyvia, I'm going to go grab something an aisle over. Murrae's right behind you."

At her assent, he turned and headed two aisles over to grab a box of diapers, which he was also nearly out of. Five minutes later, after having gotten distracted with one of the displays in the main aisle, he headed back to where he'd left the two. "Hey, are you almost—" He cut off his sentence as he glanced around. "Where's Murrae?"

"She's in the cart—" Alyvia said, glancing up at him with a confused look, but not turning around.

Tyler looked right and left, panic ballooning in his chest and painfully pushing against his ribs. "No, I said she was behind you. Were you not watching her?" He gripped her shoulder and turned her to face him. "Alyvia, where is she?!"

She looked around, a stunned look crossing her face. "I thought she was still in the cart when you left . . ."

Tyler forcefully blew out a breath and squatted down, looking under the racks where a small body could hide. "No, I took her out and left her with you. How could you let this happen? You should have been paying attention. Have you never watched a child before?" He knew his words were coming out accusatory and angry, but he didn't care right now. He needed to find Murrae.

He called her name, glancing left and right and under, conscious of Alyvia doing the same. Scenarios popped in and out of his head, quicker than he had time to dwell on, none of them pretty. He knew the statistics of kidnapped children, and he tried to push that knowledge away as terror gripped him. If she had been kidnapped . . . she could be out in the parking lot by now.

No. It was likely she just wandered off. They just had to keep looking.

After several eternal minutes, he found her two aisles over, pointing to toys hanging on the wall and jabbering with a concerned woman who had her own child clinging to her waist.

He jogged up to her and knelt down, heaving out a breath. "Murrae. Baby. You scared me." He pulled her to his chest and clung to her, inhaling her scent as she squirmed, trying to break free from his tight hold. She had absolutely no concept of the wave of emotions he had just ridden. Still holding her tightly, he pushed to his feet.

"Thank you." He addressed the woman.

She gave him an understanding smile. "No problem. Just glad she's where she belongs again. Have a good day."

"Thanks, you too," he said as she retreated down the aisle. Kissing Murrae's head, he pulled back to look at her, as if needing to convince himself that she truly was okay. She played with the button on his collar, then looked up at him with a cheeky grin.

"Dada. 'Appy." She patted his cheeks with her tiny hands, then poked her tiny finger to his lips.

As he smiled, her own grew bigger. He loved this little human so much, he sometimes thought his heart would burst. She was so in tune with his emotions, and was happiest when he was "'appy," no matter the circumstances.

Then he remembered Alyvia.

He hurried back the way he came, knowing he owed her an apology. If anything, he was more to blame for the whole thing. He should have been more careful to make sure she was aware of where Murrae was, instead of just leaving. She wasn't a parent. He shouldn't have blindly trusted her. The whole situation was his fault. Nausea churned in his stomach as he berated himself.

He found her near where they had parted, and one look at her face had guilt gnawing at his conscience. She looked like she was about to cry. Relief melted across her face as she saw him, and she hurried toward them.

"Murrae! Oh, you found her! Tyler, I'm so sorry. I feel awful—"

He held up a hand and shook his head, cutting off her apology. "No, I'm sorry, Alyvia. This was my fault. I shouldn't have gotten upset with you. I'm sorry."

She bit her lip, anxiety in her dark brown eyes.

"All's well that ends well." He smiled, and she was standing so close, he shifted and wrapped his arm around her shoulders in a brief half-hug. Then he addressed his daughter. "Well, should we go home, miss? I think that's enough adventuring today for one so small."

Alyvia laughed and grabbed the cart as Murrae said, "'Ome?"

Alyvia turned to Tyler as he pulled into the church parking lot where she had left her car, still remorseful over the situation earlier. *How could I be so irresponsible?* She had been entrusted with the care of a child, and she hadn't even been paying attention. "Ty, I really am sorry about Murrae. I feel horrible. I should have been paying better attention."

He glanced over at her before pulling into a parking space. "Please, Alyvia. Like I said, it's okay. I'm more at fault than you are. Everyone makes mistakes, and I'm just glad this one turned out okay. Don't even think about it anymore."

She pursed her lips. "Okay. If you say so."

"I say so." He winked as he shifted into park.

"Thanks, Tyler." She smiled and patted his arm still resting on the wheel. "See ya."

"Yep," he called as she closed the door and strode across the lot toward her car. She climbed in and inserted the key, just then noticing he still waited in his truck, watching her, making sure she was good before he left.

She smiled. That was sweet.

She'd never had a male figure in her life that had cared about her in such a way. Her brothers were protective, yes. But they were her brothers, so they practically had to be. She knew they truly cared about her . . . but they didn't show it as much. It was just how they were. She waved and then buckled her seat belt. Tyler, though, made her feel cared for in a more tangible way as he watched out for her, grabbed the door for her, and even as he helped in the bookstore. Like he . . . cared about her. The realization made her lungs lock, and she glanced in the rearview mirror at his truck behind her as she pulled out of the parking lot, not able to see his face due to the glare on his windshield.

She wasn't exactly sure what to do with that realization and didn't want to think about it enough to determine if it was true or not.

A wave of exhaustion swept over her as she pointed her car in the direction of home. She was very much looking forward to some thoughtful alone time.

Chapter Seventeen

Tyler slung an arm across the seat as he looked out the back window while backing out of the apartment driveway. He cast a quick look at Murrae. "All right, my little 'Rae of sunshine, you ready to hit the road?"

"Da!"

"We'll take that as a yes," he said as he accelerated down the road and headed toward I-5 South. They were finally going to Seattle. He hadn't seen his parents since they had driven up for Christmas, so he was actually very much looking forward to this trip. They may not have always seen eye to eye on every matter, but he loved his parents and they had always tried their best to be supportive of him. They had loved Sabrina like a daughter and always bemoaned the fact that they didn't often get to see their granddaughter. It would be a good weekend for them all.

As he merged onto the interstate a few minutes later, he heard Murrae's little voice from the back seat and glanced in the rearview mirror to see her face. "Dance? Dance?" she asked, wiggling in her seat.

He chuckled. Her favorite part of car rides was the music. "Okay, we can dance." He took his eyes off the road for a brief second to hit play on the album, *Rivers in the Wasteland*, he'd already queued up before they left. The music blared through the speakers of his truck and a giant grin found Murrae's face, bringing one to his own.

Clearly, she had inherited his love of music.

He bobbed his head and thumped his thumb on the wheel in time to the beat as they continued down the road.

This weekend was going to be good for them. A chance to get away, relax . . . and think.

They pulled into his parents' driveway a little before noon. They'd made good time, despite more than one stop for Murrae's sake. She was a trooper though, and had made the hour-and-a-half plus trip fairly well, all things considered. He pushed open the truck door, slid out, and pulled open the back. "You ready to see Mumsie and Popa, 'Rae?"

She looked up at him and reached her arms out, clearly ready to be out of the car seat. "Mums?"

He chuckled. She and her car seat were covered in animal cracker crumbs, the small crackers being the perfect combination of toy and snack to keep her entertained. He unbuckled her straps and lifted her out, brushing the crumbs off her new outfit as he did so. Reaching back in, he grabbed her pink diaper bag, slung it over his shoulder, and shut the door.

Because yes, he had a pink diaper bag. Sabrina had wanted all things pink for their little girl, and while he had put in a vote for a neutral color, she had, of course, won out.

Using the pink bag now only made him smile at his wife's girly-girl side.

Murrae squirmed in his arms, so he put her down, took her hand, and headed toward the front door of the dark-green, two-story home. His parents weren't wealthy by any means, but they lived comfortably enough. He reached the door and depressed the doorbell. A moment later, the door was flung wide open.

"Tyler!"

He grinned as his mom pulled him into a tight hug, and he bent down to return it. Man, he'd missed her. She hugged him for several seconds, then pulled back to look at him, cupping his face in her small, soft hands.

"How are you doing?" she asked, and he knew it wasn't just your trite, standard greeting. She wanted the truth.

"I'm doing good, Ma." He smiled.

She searched his eyes—the same blue as her own—intently for a long moment before she nodded and patted his cheek, as if needing to decide for herself that he truly was doing well. "Now. Where's my Murrae?"

Tyler looked down at where the little girl clung to his leg, and his mom squatted down in front of her. Big blue eyes looked back up at them. "'Rae, it's Mumsie." He nudged her forward slightly.

Murrae stared at his mom, head tilted. "Mums?"

Mom brushed Murrae's hair out of her face. "Hi, precious one. It's been too long, hasn't it? Gosh, Ty, she's cuter in person than on FaceTime."

He chuckled and watched as his mom held out her arms and Murrae willingly went into them for a hug. Still holding the toddler, Mom stood and led the way into the house.

"Where's Dad?" he asked, following her to the kitchen.

"Oh, he'll be here any minute. He had an errand to run. You both are probably hungry for lunch, aren't you?"

Tyler's stomach rumbled at that moment, and she chuckled. "I'll take that as a yes. You may have a few more lines on your face, but clearly some things never change." She winked at him.

He rubbed his forehead—he had lines on his face?—and chuckled sheepishly. "You got that right. Murrae here has had enough animal crackers for both of us, but I haven't eaten since breakfast before heading out."

"Well, we can fix that. I even made lemon bread this morning." She bustled about the kitchen, pulling items out of the refrigerator, Murrae perched on her hip. He didn't think she would put the little girl down until forced to do so. His mom was a tiny dynamo, her shape and height petite, but her personality was more than big

128

enough to make up for it. Her brown hair was graying slightly, and there were fine lines around her eyes, but he didn't think she looked old enough to be his mother.

"Aw, Ma, stop. So that's the amazingness I smell. Can we do dessert first?"

She gave him a mom look. "Protein first, you know the drill."

He laughed. "Clearly other things never change," he said, parroting her words back at her. She had always been a stickler for nutrition, and it was actually comforting to know that despite the turmoil and change of the years since he had left home, his mom had stayed his mom—in every way, shape, and form.

He heard a door bang and couldn't help but grin. His dad had always had a bad habit of slamming doors. "Guess Dad's home."

His mom chuckled, and he turned to be engulfed in a bear hug.

"Tyler."

"Dad. It's good to see you. It's been too long."

"You got that right." His dad slapped his back and pulled away. Michael Collens cut an imposing figure. Nearly as tall as his son, he had a face weathered by time, blond hair turning white that was perpetually too long, and broad shoulders. "Now. Where's that granddaughter of mine?"

"Hey, she's my granddaughter too, Mick," Mom teased, possessively hugging Murrae.

"Well, I see you've already gotten a few hugs in, so it's my turn." Dad stole a kiss from Mom, then turned to Murrae. "Hey, precious girl. Come give Popa a hug."

He held out his arms, and they all watched to see what the little girl would do

"Pop!" The toddler lunged for her grandpa. Though it had been a few months since she'd seen her grandparents, clearly she recognized him from pictures and video calls. His dad wrapped the little girl in his arms against his chest and she was nearly swallowed up by his large frame.

"How's my girl?" he said, kissing her cheek.

"I thought I was your girl." The teasingly sarcastic feminine voice had Tyler turning around yet again. A willowy and undeniably pretty woman set her purse on a side table and joined the group.

"Talia," he said in surprise. His sister wrapped her arms around his waist in a hug, and he reciprocated.

"Hey, big brother. Don't feel like you have to visit so often or anything. We're gonna get bored of you." She pulled out of his hug with a grin and punched his shoulder lightly. Her tendency toward sarcasm had become their love language—almost.

"Oh, sorry," he said, "I won't come back until Christmas then. Nice to know we're missed, baby sis." He lightly poked her side, and she scowled and slapped his hand away before turning to kiss both parents on the cheek.

"Something smells good." Talia inhaled deeply. "Can we eat? You know that's the only reason I came."

Their visit had been full of laughter, good food, and deep conversations. Tyler hadn't realized how much he'd missed this—this camaraderie amongst family—

until he had come back. Yes, he had his close friends in Arlington, but that couldn't replace the relationships between him and his family.

Sunday afternoon, hours before leaving, he and his mom sat on the front porch swing, listening to the peaceful sounds of cicadas, birds, quiet traffic noises, and neighborhood children playing. Talia—who had stuck around most of the weekend—and his dad watched Murrae in the house, and, from the belly laughs that floated through the window, were probably wearing the child out. Hopefully she would sleep for the drive home.

After a few moments of silence, Mom scooted closer to him on the swing and leaned against him. He put his arm across the back of the swing and around her shoulders.

"How are you really doing, Ty?" she asked.

He took a deep breath and gave it some thought before answering, knowing she wouldn't take a pat answer anyway. "I think . . . I'm actually doing pretty good, Mom. It's been . . . easier, lately. You know? Like it's not as hard to think about her, and the ache isn't as all-encompassing." He placed his fist against his chest, and her hand covered his own. "I still miss her—a lot. But I feel ready to . . . I don't know, I hate the words 'moving on.'" He snorted. "That sounds like forgetting. Like saying goodbye all over again." He shook his head, staring down at his lap. "I never wanted to say goodbye. I never thought I'd have to."

"I know," she whispered, empathy and understanding filling the two words.

He withdrew his hand from under hers and scrubbed it across his head. "You know, a couple of weeks ago I felt like God told me it was okay. It was okay to let go. But . . . I just don't know if I know how."

He felt his mom's nod against his shoulder. "Letting go doesn't have to be 'moving on' or saying goodbye. You know when you said goodbye in that hospital room, it wasn't permanent. It was just . . . goodbye for now."

"I know." He was quiet for a moment, thinking again of those last minutes. "I never told you this, but . . . Sabrina made me promise something."

"I know."

He craned his neck to look down at her, but she just shrugged, a small smile playing on her lips. "Mother's intuition."

"Oookay. She made me promise I wouldn't spend the rest of my life 'miserable and alone.' Her words." He chuckled dryly. "Do I look miserable and alone to you?"

Mom sat up and looked him over carefully. "Hmm, alone, yes, but only borderline miserable," she said in mock seriousness.

"Oh, come on. I am not." He chuckled.

She settled against his shoulder again. "So is all this to say you've found someone?"

He paused, pursing his lips and thinking of an appropriate way to respond.

"Tyler Levi, you don't know the amount of restraint I'm using to not react right now. Who is it?"

He chuckled somewhat nervously. "Who said it was anyone?"

"Your silence."

"Hmm." He hesitated again. "I don't know, Ma. Is it a coincidence that God told me to let go after I met her?"

She laughed softly. "Probably not."

"She's really nice."

"Nice?" He could hear the raised eyebrows in the tone of her voice.

"Okay, she's pretty, funny, smart, kind, gentle, and adores Murrae. And Murrae adores her." He paused. "Murrae called her 'mom' the other day."

He felt her stiffen slightly. "Why?"

"I'm still trying to figure that out. She knows Sabrina by 'mama.' I almost never use the word 'mom.'"

"How did that make you feel?" He could hear the wariness in her voice and understood the protectiveness in it.

"Honestly? My lungs locked up for a second." He laughed. "I was just so shocked. Alyvia gently corrected her and laughed it off, but I think she understood."

His mom leaned away to look up at him with a smug look on her face.

"What?"

"I got a name. Alyvia Emmerson?"

He groaned and gave a rueful shake of his head. "You sneak. Yes, you're correct."

She nodded thoughtfully. "Piper's friend, right?"

He made a sound of assent.

"So what are you going to do about it?"

"About what?" he asked mischievously.

She angled another "mom look" his way. "It." She paused, and when he didn't respond, added, "Just don't wait too long. I know you're ready. In here." She patted his chest. "Don't second guess yourself."

He gave a slow nod, serious now. "Thanks, Ma." He leaned in to kiss her cheek. "Pray for me?" he asked softly, his voice catching.

She smiled gently and cupped her hand against his cheek. "Always, honey."

Never Say Goodbye

Chapter Eighteen

Alyvia folded her arms and stared at the brick
picture window facade on E. 5th Street. A
metal sign hung parallel to the building with the words
Happy Haven Books engraved on it in a bold yet
whimsical font. She'd paid a fortune for that custom
sign, but she wanted something unique to catch a
passerby's eye.

But despite the sign and the engaging window
setting, something didn't feel quite right. She wanted
the storefront to portray a warm and inviting aesthetic,
but it still lacked . . . something. At least to her eye.

She reentered the store, the bell ringing its cheery
hello, and started rearranging the bookshelf set in the
window. Finally, she paused and snapped her fingers.

"Light!"

Old Mrs. Cramer's head poked up from across the
store where she was browsing the memoir titles. Alyvia

135

gave a smile and waved her off, then said more softly to herself, "I need more light." The window was too dark to give off the warm atmosphere she'd been trying to achieve. How did she not see it before now?

She scrambled off the ledge that set the window display apart from the rest of the store and hurried behind the front desk, wiggling the mouse on the computer to bring it to life. A quick search and she found what she was looking for. She added the items to her cart, checked out, and *viola!* Thank goodness for Amazon Prime. The package would be delivered tomorrow. That was practically faster than she could go to a store to buy them.

Mrs. Cramer was ready to check out by the time she finished. The lady certainly kept Happy Haven in business thanks to her frequent patronage. Alyvia rang up her purchase and sent her on her way with a cheery smile and a "Have a nice day!"

A mumble was all she got in response, but at least she had made eye contact this time. That was an improvement.

The bell on the door sang out its cheery note again as it opened and shut behind the older woman, and Alyvia dug through the items strewn across the counter to find her phone. She pressed one of the numbers on the favorites list and put it to her ear.

A few rings, then, "'Ello?"

"Tyler! I'm going to need your help hanging up some Christmas lights."

"Lyv, it's—" a pause, as if he was checking the calendar, "April. You're several months early. Or late, however you look at it."

She laughed. "True enough. But I just bought some super nice ones on Amazon, and I want to hang them in the windows in front of the store. They'll look so nice and make it look so cozy!"

He gave a chuckle. "Sorry, Alyvia. But I'm hardcore team No Christmas Before Thanksgiving, so I don't think I can help you." Even through the phone, she heard the mock seriousness in his voice. Or was it mock seriousness?

She paused. "You're joking, right?"

"Nah, I'm dead serious. I can't even touch Christmas-related items until after Thanksgiving. Makes Christmas shopping a bit tight each year, but I've made it work this long."

Alyvia burst out laughing. "You don't even buy Christmas gifts before Thanksgiving?"

"Not even kidding!" She heard the earnestness in his voice. "Ask anyone who knows me. I'm strict-strict. Like, hardcore."

"So, gingerbread?"

"Nope."

"No Peppermint Mochas?"

"I hate peppermint, but nope."

"No . . ." She wracked her brain for more Christmas. "No Christmas music, prolly. Not even Josh Groban's 'Thankful'? That's basically a Thanksgiving song!"

"Nope. Love Josh Groban's Christmas album though. Just in season."

"You love Josh Groban too?"

He laughed. "Well, mostly just his Christmas album. But his voice is crazy awesome."

"No one else I know likes his music! Anyway, we're getting off topic. So no snow and ice, ice skating, or icicles either?"

A chuckle. "Okay, even you have to admit you're pushing it a bit. Ice and snow is just a winter thing, not a Christmas thing. Plus I can't control the weather."

She shook her head, grinning. "You're a weirdo."

"I've been called worse." For the first time, she heard the amusement and humor trickling through the phone.

"You're pulling my leg, aren't you," she said, not really asking because she knew he was.

He blew out a sigh. "All right, I'm pulling your leg. But in my defense, half of this conversation was true. I am pretty hardcore about no Christmas before Thanksgiving, but I'm not so hardcore not to help a damsel in distress hang up some Christmas lights. But for the sake of saving face, can we call them twinkle lights?"

She laughed. "Deal. You help me hang up my lights, and we can call them twinkle lights."

He laughed too, and she liked the sound. She liked Tyler. He was a goof and drove her a bit crazy sometimes, but . . . she liked him.

"Well, I gotta go. Murrae is yelling at me from her car seat, so I better take a snack break. We're on our way home from Seattle."

"Oh! Sorry. I'll let you go then."

"Don't be sorry, it was a good distraction. It gets a bit lonely being the only adult in the car on road trips. You start to lose your sanity after singing 'The Wheels on the Bus' ninety-eight times."

She laughed. "All right. Drive safe."

"Will do. Text me when you want me to hang up the lights. I think I'm free most evenings this week."

"Will do," she parroted back. "Bye."

"Bye, Lyv."

She hung up and looked at her phone. She didn't know when he'd started calling her Lyv. Maybe somewhere around the time she started calling him Ty.

Don't overthink it.

She was horribly good at overthinking. Setting aside the phone with a smile, she looked up and greeted a group of high school girls who had just walked in, saying a silent prayer of safety for Tyler as he drove.

And safety for her heart, too.

Chapter Nineteen

"It's okay, baby, we're home. We're home," Tyler said into the darkened rearview mirror of the truck. Murrae had been fussing, then outright crying, for the last half hour of the drive. Snacks, toys, pacifier, music—nothing soothed her. She had reached over-tired, which was also known as *the point of no return*. He knew from experience that a bath, PJs, and bed was the only remedy at this point. He pulled into his spot in the apartment parking lot and put the truck in park. Opening the back door, he unbuckled the straps holding Murrae in place and lifted her out. She promptly laid her head on his shoulder and wiped her tears and snot on his t-shirt.

"Nice," he mumbled. But at least she'd stopped crying. He patted her back, then reached in to grab her bag. Shutting the door and clicking the lock button on his fob, he shoved the keys into his pocket and headed up the stairs to his apartment. He'd run back down to grab his own duffel after Murrae was asleep.

His jaw nearly cracked in a yawn as he climbed the stairs. Just listening to Murrae cry had exhausted him. Brushing her tangled hair back, he pressed a kiss to her red and sweaty face. Her eyelids drooped with exhaustion. Maybe just a warm washcloth instead of a bath would expedite the bedtime process.

By the time he laid her in her crib, she was out like a light. He blew out a breath of relief and closed the door to her room partway, feeling again the wet spot on his shoulder from where she'd wiped her face. Grimacing, he grabbed a tissue and scrubbed at it. *Gross.* Hurrying back down the steps, he grabbed his bag from the truck and hurried back up. Another yawn stretched his jaw. *He* needed to get to bed. People made traveling sound so restful, but as nice as the weekend had been, based on how he felt now, he wouldn't call it restful. Although, maybe those people didn't travel with a toddler.

He unpacked, showered, and found a clean uniform for tomorrow—practically a miracle—and collapsed onto the couch by 9:30. He stabbed the TV remote's on button and found a game to watch.

But he found his mind wandering back to his phone conversation with Alyvia on the way home. He grinned. It was almost too fun to tease her. She was a good sport about it, but he could tell she sometimes wasn't sure if he actually was teasing or not. She'd get this hesitant, serious tone, as if she thought he was teasing but didn't want to offend him if he was serious. It was cute.

His grin faded, his eyes not processing the baseball game happening on TV anymore. Was it right to tease her like that? Over the past several weeks, they'd developed quite the friendship. A comfortable friendship. But was it too comfortable? He enjoyed her company, and he liked her . . . really liked her. But if it couldn't be more than that, he didn't want to play with her emotions.

But could it be more than a comfortable friendship?

Did he want it to be more than a friendship?

The hard knot in his chest screamed, *No!*

He wanted to believe in second chances, and he knew Sabrina did . . . But everything would be more complicated this time than it had been with Sabrina.

Nothing had been complicated at all with Sabrina Richards. They'd met at a fundraiser the hospital had put on and discovered they had mutual friends. She was a classic beauty with her wavy dark hair, bright brown eyes, and a nose dotted with adorable freckles. He sighed. Yes, her beauty had struck him first, but it was *her* that stuck with him. He had found himself watching her over the course of the night, and while she was very quiet, her sweet spirit and kind and genuine personality had been clear. He'd recognized right away that she wasn't just beautiful on the outside, it was the inside that was as well. She volunteered in the pediatric ward, and after that night, he'd sweet-talked a nurse into inadvertently mentioning what hours she worked. The older lady hadn't stopped going on about how great Sabrina was. He smiled at the memory.

Over the next several weeks, he had conveniently found himself in the peds unit when Sabrina happened to be there. Until she called him out on it. She was introverted and quiet, but she was spunky too. He asked her out, and within weeks, he found he'd gone from noticing her, to liking her, to *really* liking her, to finding himself in love with her.

He just had to convince her of that, but within six months of meeting, they were engaged. And he'd never stopped loving her.

Will I ever stop? There wasn't anything as pure and wonderful as first love.

But as he found out eventually, love was painful too. When they'd exchanged vows, he'd assumed the sickness in the phrase "in sickness and in health" was the flu, or maybe old age.

But it was holding her hair and stroking her back as she vomited over the toilet endlessly, from morning sickness, or so they'd thought. But when it didn't end, they eventually realized it was the cancer. It was holding her as she tried to sleep through horrible migraines when the only place she was comfortable was on his chest. It was steadying her when she stumbled from the dizziness. It was endless doctor appointments in countless cities and more days in the hospital than out.

Tyler pressed his fingers to his eyes. In the end, it was "death do us part" far sooner than he'd ever imagined.

As excruciating and overwhelming as the pain he'd faced, he had no idea how Sabrina had faced the pain she'd experienced, which was without a doubt far more than he had. And yet she was still so calm about it all.

Love was wonderful, beautiful, and glorious. Love was pain, loss, and devastation.

And as much as he wanted to believe in second chances, as much as he wanted a second chance . . .

He mindlessly flicked the remote at the TV to change the channel as a commercial came on. The thought of walking through that kind of pain again made him want to run screaming in the other direction.

Tyler jolted awake to the shrill buzzing of the doorbell. He was on the couch, the TV was playing the morning news, and he had a crick in his neck so bad he could barely move it. He groaned. Apparently he never made it to bed last night.

The shrill buzzing came again, and he stumbled to his feet, trying to relax his shoulder muscles that were strung tighter than a drum from the uncomfortable way he'd lain on the couch for—he checked his watch and groaned again as he reached the door—eight and a half hours. He was so going to be late for work.

He pulled open the door for Ellen, still rubbing his neck. Her eyebrows raised as she saw him. "Good morning. Sorry. I overslept."

"I can see that," she said with a small smile.

He shut the door behind her, then turned toward his room. "I've got to get a move on. Murrae's still sleeping."

"I'll brew you some coffee."

"Thanks," he called over his shoulder as he shut the door behind himself. He was grateful to have found someone to take care of Murrae who treated them like the family she didn't have. He hurriedly dressed and shoved a change of clothes into his duffel before entering the adjoining bathroom. He didn't have time to shave the weekend-long stubble on his face, but he brushed his teeth and ran a wet comb through his hair. He needed a haircut too.

He rushed, and he was ready ten minutes before he had to leave. He dropped his duffel by the door and blew out a breath. Rushing around to be out the door for work stressed him out. Ellen handed him a mug of coffee, and he gratefully took it and gulped a few mouthfuls of the hot brew, wishing it were espresso.

Tyler massaged the side of his neck with his free hand, grimacing at the pain. He was going to dig out that chiropractor's business card and make an appointment for tonight or tomorrow. Ellen noticed, and she pulled out a chair at the table and sat, pointing to the floor at her feet.

"Sit."

"Huh?" He stopped rubbing his shoulder.

"Sit. I'll rub your shoulders for a few minutes. You'll feel better. You have a few minutes yet."

He'd shrug, but that would hurt, so he sat on the floor in front of her, and her hands massaged his shoulders and neck. It hurt, but he knew it was helping. After a few minutes, he pushed to his feet. "Thanks, Ellen. What would we do without you?" He poured more coffee into a travel mug.

Ellen snorted. "Not much, that's what."

"So true." He threw his duffel over his shoulder and pulled open the door. "See you tonight. Give 'Rae a kiss for me." She was usually up before he left, and he missed his goodbye kiss.

"I will. Have a good day."

As it was, Tyler strode into the station only a few minutes late. Not bad for sleeping well past when his alarm should have gone off—had he set it. Ezra spotted him and waved, then raised a brow as he drew closer.

"Dude. Rough night?"

Tyler made a face. "Something like that. Man, my neck is killing me. Apparently my body is getting way too old to sleep on the couch."

"Why—?" Ezra frowned, then shook his head, apparently deeming it wiser not to ask.

Which was good, because Tyler did not want to discuss his thoughts from last night. Best friend or no, he wasn't ready to go there. Ezra would push. Granted, it would be in a good-natured way and with only the best of intentions.

But Tyler didn't need pushing right now.

Ezra smacked Tyler's shoulder instead. "You're becoming such an old man."

Tyler breathed out a chuckle and pulled his phone off his belt as an incoming text vibrated. It was Ellen.

"Was Murrae sick last night?"

He frowned. *"No?"* Then a second text, *"Why?"* Then, *"Is she okay?"*

Ellen seemed to take too long to text him back, and he stared at his phone, waiting. Finally, *"She has a runny nose and is a tiny bit feverish. She's fine, I'll keep an eye on her."*

Tyler pursed his lips. Murrae had been an incredibly healthy girl, considering her early birth. *"Keep me updated plz."*

"Ty? Everything okay?"

He looked up to find Ezra watching him. He put his phone back onto the clip on his belt and took a swig of coffee from his travel mug. "Yeah. Murrae is coming down with something, I guess."

Ezra made a face. "Well, that's fun."

"Yeah." Tyler checked his phone again. *Babies get sick all the time. Murrae's fine. Chill out, man.* But he wished he were there so he could know for sure.

Chapter Twenty

Alyvia leaned against the counter of her bookstore and stared at her phone, chewing her lip. Her dad's appearance at the bookstore two weeks ago had started a tentative and reluctant text thread between the two of them. He would ask a question about the store, or about a book, and they'd text. Briefly. Just surface talk.

At least it was something, she told herself.

She couldn't remember anymore why she wanted to stay angry at him. The anger, the bitterness toward him was dissipating. Was everything happy and dandy? Far from it.

But she knew she was on the right track.

And now?

She reread the new text from him, asking her to join him for dinner tonight. He'd hinted at wanting to see her again, but hadn't shown up at the bookstore again, thankfully respecting her need for space. But now he'd finally asked.

That uncomfortable feeling when she just *really* didn't want to do something swirled through her chest. She blew out a breath, then hit the icon with her mom's face in the phone app.

Her mom's response was predictable. "It's just one dinner, honey. Why is that so bad?"

"I don't know, Mom. It's just . . . I don't know. It's awkward. What on earth are we going to talk about?"

"Alyvia." She could hear the mild scolding in her mother's tone. "You'll think of something. It doesn't have to be as complicated as you're making it in your head. You're overthinking it."

She sighed. Mom was right.

Mom continued in a softer, gentler tone. "I know how you feel, Alyvia. I do. I understand. But you don't have to be afraid. He . . . he's changed."

Alyvia gnawed on her thumbnail. "Who said anything about being afraid?"

"You're afraid he won't be different. And if he is different, you're afraid he'll leave again. You're afraid to be let down. You don't want to get your hopes up only to be disappointed. You're afraid, Alyvia."

She was quiet for several seconds. She would have never thought those things about herself, but . . . every single one resonated in that splintered and bruised place deep within her.

"Alyvia?"

"You're right, Mom," she whispered, her voice cracking.

She heard a sympathetic tsk over the line. "Aw, honey. It's okay. I promise. Everything will be okay. God . . . I feel like God is restoring our family." Her mom's voice had become hushed and choked. "I've prayed so, so long for this. Please, Alyvia. Talk with your dad."

Alyvia swallowed back the tears that rose, and once again she was reminded that she wasn't the only one affected in this situation. She wasn't the only one hurting. "I'll text him."

Her mom sniffed and audibly swallowed. "Thank you, baby. I love you."

"I love you too, Mom," she said softly before hanging up.

Alyvia put her car in park and took a deep breath. In through the nose, out through the mouth. Her left heel tapped on the floorboard as her leg jiggled. She blew out another breath and swiped the loose strands of hair back from her face.

"God, I don't want to do this," she whispered under her breath.

You need to sometime, so why not get it over with?

Alyvia got out of her car and locked it. It still felt so intimidating. It was her father, not some stranger or creep. But he was a stranger to her. What would they talk about? Would the whole night just be awkward silence? You could only talk about the weather or food for so long.

She pulled open the door to the restaurant, entered, and was directed to a table in the back corner. The area was lit by windows on both sides. Thankfully, the restaurant was more than half empty, and the bright lights created a cozy atmosphere. Her father was seated at the table and looked up as she walked closer, quickly pushing to his feet when he saw her.

"Alyvia. Hi." He smiled at her and stood there, seeming unsure how to proceed.

Well, she could manage a hug. She leaned in for a half-hug, and though he seemed surprised, he wrapped his arm around her shoulders, squeezing gently. She smiled back as she pulled away and took a seat directly across from the one he had chosen.

A waitress appeared and took her drink order before disappearing again.

"How are you doing?" Dad asked the rote question, his fingers playing with the straw in his water glass. *He's nervous as well.* Good. At least that made two of them.

"I'm well. How are you?" she said with a small smile.

"Good, good." He nodded, then picked up his menu. "Do you know what you want to order?"

She picked up hers as well. "Um, no, I've never been here before," she said, perusing the menu for something to pique her interest.

"Well, I've only been here a few times, but their New York Strip and steak fries are pretty good. You like steak, right?" He looked up at her, as if realizing he didn't know her much at all.

The feeling is mutual. "I love steak. I guess I'll have that." She set the menu aside and folded her hands.

He smiled and did the same. "I'll have that too, then." They gave their orders to the waitress and after a few uncomfortable starts and stops, they managed small talk until their food arrived. Automatically, Alyvia started to bow her head to say a silent, quick prayer over her food, but as she did, she noticed her dad doing the same, almost a second before she did. He asked a blessing over their food and conversation in a short prayer, then picked up his knife and fork.

Well, that was kind of awkward. Alyvia didn't know why she felt surprised by it but she picked up a steak fry and ate it. Delicious.

They continued with conversation about everyday life, both getting to know each other as if they were new friends.

In a way, they were. Or, very old friends who hadn't seen each other in ten years.

Alyvia found herself relaxing as minutes ticked into an hour. This actually wasn't so bad, and she was even somewhat enjoying it. Plus, she got a free dinner out of the deal. Although she mentally smacked herself for that crass thought.

After the waitress took their dishes, there were a few moments of silence, although it wasn't as uncomfortable or tense as it had been at the start of the night. But as she took a sip of her water, Alyvia noticed her father fidgeting with his napkin. She swallowed and set her glass down, waiting for him to say something.

Finally, he did, reluctantly looking up to meet her eyes. "Alyvia . . . I . . . I'm just going to say it. I would like to apologize for . . . the past. For leaving." He held a hand up. "I know what you're thinking, an apology is just words, but I want to prove to you that I'm sincere, if you'll let me." He paused and searched her face, as if asking permission to continue.

She bit her cheek and gave a small jerk of her head that constituted a nod.

He reached across the table and took her hand in both of his. They were rough and calloused but held hers gently. He blew out a breath. "Alyvia Faye . . . I'm sorry. I'm sorry for leaving, but before that, I'm sorry for not being the father you needed. You deserved a much better man than me for a father, and I'm so sorry I couldn't be that for you. I'm sorry for every moment of hurt, abandonment, and fear I caused you. And I'm sorry—" His voice rasped and he swallowed repeatedly, struggling to finish his sentence. "I'm sorry if my poor example ever made you doubt how your heavenly Father loves you." He looked up at her, eyes red and watery. Her own eyes stung. "I'm so sorry, Alyvia. I just wish I had the chance to do it all over again. I want you to know that even though I showed it horribly, I loved you—and each of your siblings—with all of me. I *do* love you with all of me."

"Then why did you leave?" The words blurted out before she could stop them. But she didn't regret them.

Dad swiped the back of his hand across his eyes and took a deep breath, looking as if he was searching for words. "For a lot of my adult years, I dealt with depression. I wasn't diagnosed until later, and there wasn't a lot of information on clinical depression when I was in my twenties. I had my good times and my bad times, but when I married your mom and you guys came along, I did really good for a lot of years. I thought I was cured, or something. But when you were little . . . it came back. And it got so bad that I started using alcohol to help me cope."

Alyvia's lungs froze and she tried not to let her shock show. But it was hard. Her father . . . had—has?—depression? He was . . . an alcoholic? Her brain had either stopped processing or was processing too fast, because she didn't know what to think, or how to react.

"It started out with just a few drinks on bad days, but eventually I started getting drunk on my worst days, which were somewhat regular." He shook his head, rubbing his hand over his mouth. "I knew it was wrong, but I had so many excuses in my head as to why it was okay. As you can imagine, the alcohol wasn't helping the depression—making it worse, actually. After a time, your mother started insisting I needed to get help . . . or I needed to leave. So I left."

She felt completely numb and frozen.

"I was too stubborn to admit I needed help, much less ask for it." Her dad stared at the table for a silent moment, his shoulders hunched. The sounds of the restaurant continued around them: dishes clinking, calls from the kitchen, conversations swirling together and creating white noise. Then he gave a humorless chuckle. "So now you know your dad was a depressed alcoholic." His voice hoarsened, and his shoulders sank even more, as if he wanted to cave in on himself, disappear.

Even though she didn't want to acknowledge it, Alyvia recognized the shame and guilt in his voice and posture. The self-hatred and even the fear. Fear of rejection. She felt torn. She wanted to forgive him, but an anger still simmered deep below the surface. Anger that he didn't care enough about himself, his family, to admit his issues and get help. He'd faced this battle alone. He'd chosen rejection, then became rejected.

But now . . .

She swallowed once, twice. Shook her head and tried to clear the fog. "Was?"

Her father looked up to meet her eyes before returning his gaze back to the wood grain of the tabletop. He cleared his throat. "Was. Eventually, I got help for the drinking. Got in touch with a really good counselor. Even tried a few different medications for the depression, but I didn't like 'em, so I stuck with counseling and therapy, which seems to have worked, for now anyway. So, was. Now . . . I want to move forward. I've missed so much. I know it's a lot to ask you to forgive me, but . . . can you just give me a second chance, Lyvy?"

Now it was her turn to stare at the tabletop. Her thoughts roared, and conflicting emotions fought for dominance. She looked up and met his eyes. Those light brown eyes that were filled with . . . shame and fear and pleading and pain.

She pushed back her chair, stood, and grabbed her purse. "I have to go," she said softly.

"Lyvy—"

She left without looking back.

Chapter Twenty-One

Tyler slipped his key into the lock on the apartment door and entered. He caught sight of Ellen sitting in the rocking recliner in the small living space, making hushing motions at him. He nodded, just catching himself before he slammed the door. Sheesh, he didn't realize he'd picked up that bad habit from his dad. Locking the door, he ditched his duffel on the couch and walked over to where Ellen sat. Murrae lay cuddled on her lap, her flushed cheeks making it look like she'd gone down with a fight.

He looked at Ellen and spoke softly. "How's she doing?"

Ellen matched her tone to his. "She's fine. Just extra fussy. She's been sniffling and coughing and had a low fever most of the day. I just got her to sleep, after a bit of screaming." She made a wry face, and Tyler understood the sentiment.

Murrae may have been born ten weeks early, but her lungs now were healthy and fully functioning.

"Thanks, Ellen. I know she can be a bit of a mini monster when she's sick." He rubbed the back of his neck and sank onto the couch. "I don't know where she could have picked up a bug from."

Ellen shook her head. "You know little ones are constantly getting sick. It's not a big deal. She'll be right as rain in a day or two."

Tyler nodded and gave a small smile. "You're right. I'll let you get home." With some careful maneuvering, Ellen shifted Murrae into Tyler's arms and left. He sank back onto the couch and pulled Murrae close against himself, gently rubbing her back. He pressed his lips to her forehead and felt the heat of her fever. Poor thing.

He held her for a few minutes more before laying her in her crib. She hardly stirred as he did so, and he figured she must be exhausted. Running his hand across her silky-soft tangled hair, he whispered a goodnight before pulling the door closed.

Stifling a yawn, he rummaged around in the pantry until he found a box of white cheddar Cheez-Its. He popped one in his mouth and chewed, then shrugged. Stale, but it was still a Cheez-It. Apparently he needed to stock up on some "adult" snacks—aka, not animal crackers and puffs. As evidenced by the toys and toddler items in his living room and the food in his kitchen, his life was all but consumed with the little girl sleeping in her room. He missed the close companionship of another adult. Yes, he saw Ezra and others when he worked, but it wasn't the same.

He missed Sabrina. He missed falling asleep and waking up next to her. He missed sharing his life, his heart, and whatever was on his mind with his closest friend, his other half. He missed being married and felt cheated out of the opportunity to raise their child together.

He leaned on the kitchen countertop and stuck his hand in the box of crackers, not even bothering to pour them into a bowl. "Aw, God, I miss her so much," he muttered.

Or do you miss what you had?

He paused at the thought, a cracker halfway to his mouth. Did he miss what he had instead of just missing Sabrina?

Somewhere along the way, the grief of losing her had lessened . . . and he was left with loneliness.

Yes. He missed his life, what he'd had. It had been robbed from him by a ruthless thief named Death. Of course he missed Sabrina, his first love, and he didn't think he'd ever stop missing her and grieving his loss.

But missing and grieving never brought someone back from the dead.

You can move on. You can have hope.

His mind immediately went to Alyvia. She was full of dreams, of life, of light. Of hope.

The familiar pang of guilt surfaced, but he shoved it away.

You can move on. You can have hope.

Hope.

"Our God is the God of second chances, Tyler. Find your second chance. I don't want you to become a lonely old man. You'd make a crotchety old man." She smiled at him. Oh, that smile.

But he couldn't smile back. "How can you talk like that, 'Brina? I love you. *I've only* ever *loved you." He leaned in to kiss her, but she caught his chin, stopping him and forcing him to meet her eyes.*

"I love you, too, Ty, and I love you for that. But someday when someone catches your eye, I need you to know it's okay to love again. I need you to know that."

He couldn't talk around the emotion squeezing at his throat, so he leaned in again and pressed his lips to hers, lingering. She let him this time, and kissed him back, her palm against his cheek. Then her hand moved to his shoulder and she pushed him back a few inches, pleading with those melted chocolate eyes.

"Please, Tyler. I need you to understand. Tell me you hear me." Her voice was choked and tears slipped past her lashes, her composure shattering, his own long gone.

He rested his forehead against hers, his breathing ragged. "I hear you. I hear you."

A droplet hit the counter and Tyler started. His cheeks were wet. He swiped his sleeve across his face and blew out a deep breath. Dumping the box of crackers onto the countertop, he picked out the rest of the whole crackers and ate them before sweeping the crummy remnants into the garbage can.

Dropping onto the couch, he turned the TV on and channel surfed for a solid five minutes before pulling his phone from his pocket. He checked the time; not even 9:30 yet. He opened up his contacts, his finger hovered over the call icon for five seconds—he counted—before he pressed it and waited as it rang.

Alyvia picked up her buzzing phone and hesitated when she saw the name on the screen. Then swiped to answer it. "Tyler, hi."

"Hey, Alyvia. How was your day?" His voice sounded . . . different.

And he was calling to ask about her day? She started to smile, but it faded when she remembered her day. "It was . . . interesting, to say the least."

"Interesting in a good way or bad?"

"To be honest, I . . . I don't know yet."

She could sense his confusion. "Oookay. Want to talk about it?"

"Well, how was your day?"

He chuckled. "Okay, fine. Mine was interesting as well. Murrae caught some bug, so she's not feeling the hottest. She was asleep when I got home, but apparently she didn't go down without a fight."

Alyvia laughed softly. "She's a fighter."

"That's for sure. I'm hoping she'll sleep most of it off tonight and feel better tomorrow. Otherwise, I may stay home tomorrow. I don't want to lose the hours, but I don't want to leave her either."

"I understand. I'm sure she would be fine with Ellen, though."

"Yeah, probably." Then he gave a laugh. "I guess I hover a bit, don't I?"

She smiled. "A bit?"

"You've noticed?"

"Um, well, you don't hide it or anything." She laughed.

"Ah, fair enough." He groaned. "They say every parent tends to be overprotective of their firstborn, but . . ."

Alyvia silently nodded, knowing it was more than that.

"So." Tyler broke the moment of quiet. "What happened with you today?"

Alyvia sighed heavily. "Well . . ."

"You don't have to tell me if you don't want to."

She appreciated that, but she wanted to talk about it with someone . . . And it would be nice to get the perspective of someone else—who wasn't family. "No, it's okay. You know how I said my dad hasn't been around much, but he's back in Arlington now?"

"Yeah, I remember."

"He finally convinced me to have dinner with him tonight, and . . . well, we talked."

"That sounds like a good thing."

"It was, I guess, but . . ."

"It was hard," he filled in.

"Yeah." A few moments of silence ticked by.

"He had depression, Tyler. I guess he did when he was younger, but he was never diagnosed or anything. He said when he and Mom got married, he was doing really well for awhile, but when I was little, it got bad again. I never knew." She found herself trying not to cry.

She *really* didn't want to cry.

"Aw, I'm sorry, Lyv." Tyler's voice was full of understanding.

She cleared her throat. "He started drinking then too, and Mom told him he had to get help or leave. So he left." She took a breath. "I feel so confused now. I've been thinking one thing for so long, but I didn't know the full story. Things make more sense now, but . . . I guess I'm still angry that he chose to leave instead of staying, admitting he had a problem, and getting help."

"I understand. But his mind was messed up, Alyvia. I'm sure *he* was very confused."

"Yeah," she said. "I want to forgive him. I do. I just don't know if I can. Ugh, I feel so confused!"

"It's okay to feel confused, Alyvia. That's a lot of stuff to process all in one day. It's gonna take some time to absorb it all, and that's okay."

"Yeah. Thank you for saying that, Tyler," she said softly. She thought back over the evening. "If you could have seen his face, Tyler. He looked so . . . so ashamed. So broken. I've never seen him like that before." She paused. "I feel bad for just leaving, but . . . ."

"I'm sure it takes a lot of courage to admit something like that . . . especially to your daughter."

"Mmm." She chewed her thumbnail. "I want to forgive him."

"That's the start. You're on the right track. And Alyvia?"

"Huh?"

"You have to forgive him for yourself, if not for him. That bitterness will only eat away at your own heart until there's no light left. Trust me, you don't want that to happen."

She nodded, still gnawing on her nail. "You're right." She paused. "Who were you angry with?"

He hesitated and cleared his throat, and she almost rescinded the question.

"God," he said.

Oh. "Thanks for listening, and for the advice, Tyler. It means a lot."

"No problem. Your bill is in the mail."

She laughed. "I see how it is."

They chatted for a few minutes longer before hanging up. Alyvia plugged in her phone, then sank deeper into the corner of the small couch in her tiny living area, thinking about what he had said, that she needed to forgive her dad for herself.

He was right.

The bitterness *was* eating away at her, causing a rift in her family, poisoning her mind. She needed to forgive him, and maybe . . . maybe she owed him an apology as well.

She leaned her head back against the couch and prayed silently, asking God to forgive her for letting the bitterness take root in her heart and fill her mind. Then she stilled, smiling, feeling a sense of complete peace welling up from somewhere deep inside her.

She was actually looking forward to seeing her dad again. She knew things would still be awkward, and it would take them time to move forward . . . but she was ready to take the step.

Chapter Twenty-Two

Tyler started awake two nights later. It was still dark out, and in the sleep-induced fog, he felt disoriented. What had woken him?

A cry from the other room reached his ears. That was it.

He rolled out of bed but tripped, his foot caught in the sheet. *Jeepers.* He shook his head to clear it and hurriedly made his way to Murrae's room. He flicked the hallway light on before he entered and spotted her standing in her crib, gripping the rail and crying between hacking coughs. Yesterday it seemed like she was feeling better, but . . . "Heyyy, 'Rae, what's the matter?" She held out her arms, and he reached in to pick her up, settling her on his shoulder.

Brushing her hair back from her face, he inhaled. "Sheesh, girl." She felt hotter than a furnace. He patted her back and paced the length of the small room a few times until she quieted. He laid her on the dresser's changing pad to change her out of the fleece jammies into something cooler, but she vomited before he could even undo the zipper.

Tyler grimaced, now fully awake. "Aw, honey . . ." She fussed and coughed. "I know, I know. This is even less fun for you." He washed her face, changed her into clean pajamas, and quickly cleaned up the mess. Yawning now, he picked her up again. She rested her head against his shoulder and wrapped her arm around his neck, clinging to him with tiny whimpers and tired coughs.

His heart was a complete puddle. The loneliness and hard work of solo parenting struck him every single day, and some days were a battle not to lose his sanity. But when it came down to it . . . she was just a tiny human being, his own flesh and blood, and implicitly relied on him for her every need.

A beautiful and terrifying thing.

Because he didn't want to mess this up.

Holding her tighter, his bare feet paced the carpeted floor for a half hour before he tried to lay her back in her crib. But she only fussed more, causing her to cough until she was almost wheezing. Concern drew a tight knot in the center of his chest, and he picked her back up, trying to calm her as her crying only made the coughing worse.

He really wished he had a stethoscope right now. His brain was torn between full-on dad mode and medical professional mode. In one, he tried to fight back the fear that this could be something very bad. And in the other, he assured himself that illnesses were very common in children and she'd likely be better by morning.

Still holding her with his left arm, he dug through a cabinet in the bathroom until he found a children's fever reducer. Hopefully she wouldn't vomit it back up. Thankfully, the medicine went down without a fight— a sign she was clearly exhausted. He wet a soft cloth to place on her face and neck, then sat in the recliner in the living room.

He tried to stay awake to make sure her fever went down once the medicine kicked in, but within minutes they both were asleep.

Tyler jerked awake, then winced when the movement pulled at the tight muscles in his neck. He *needed* to stop sleeping in weird places. He checked his watch—6:21 a.m. Just a few minutes until his alarm would go off. Not that he would have heard it, given that it was in his bedroom. He looked down at Murrae, his left arm numb beneath her, and the events of the night came back to him. He vaguely remembered waking a little after two a.m. and finding that her fever had lessened.

He shook his head in an effort to clear it and pressed his palm against Murrae's neck. Hot. Her fever must have risen again after the medicine had worn off. He needed to wake her and get some fluids and more medicine into her. He paused and listened to her breathe for a moment, noticing the rasp. Her shallow breaths came quickly.

He took a deep breath and swallowed hard, trying to decide if he was panicking because that's what he did best when it came to Murrae, or if there was actually cause for it this time. He gently tried to wake her. It seemed to take forever until her eyes blinked lethargically up at him, her cheeks bright with fever.

"Aww, honeygirl . . ." He scooped her up and pressed a kiss to her too-warm cheek. Digging around in the bathroom cabinet again, he found a thermometer and took her temperature. The digital screen read 104.1.

He could feel the fear nipping at the edges of his sanity, and he fought to remain calm. Somehow, he dealt with life or death situations daily and was always able to keep his cool. But when it came to his daughter . . . he felt like he was coming apart at the seams.

He forced himself into paramedic mode. If anyone told him their young child had a fever over 103, he'd tell them to go to the ER. And with her breathing . . . He forced himself to examine her carefully and analytically noted her symptoms in his head. Her skin was pale beneath the fever flush, her breathing was rapid, shallow, and wheezing. Fever of 104. A very faint tinge of blue circling her lips told him absorbing enough oxygen was a struggle. And with having a fever on and off the last three days, she was likely headed toward dehydration, despite his attempts to force liquids into her.

"All right, baby girl, we're gonna get you feeling better, I promise," he said, tucking her hair back. She just looked up at him, looking too miserable to cry or fuss or say anything, and he felt like his heart was breaking into pieces.

Laying her on his bed, he quickly changed into clothes and slipped a pair of shoes on his feet, tucking his wallet into his back pocket and grabbing his keys. He then loaded Murrae's diaper bag and hurried out to the car with her.

As he pulled out of his parking space, he used the hands-free mode on his phone to call Ezra.

"What's up, man?"

"Hey." He took a deep breath. "I'm headed to the ER with Murrae."

"What's going on?" Ezra's voice was calm and steady. Ezra was *always* calm and steady.

Tyler tried to steal a measure of it as he explained Murrae's worsened symptoms. "I just want to get her checked out and get her some oxygen and fluids," he said, glancing in the rearview mirror at her.

"Sounds like you're making the right call. Listen, I'll call them right now and let them know you're on your way. Then I'll see who I can find to cover your shift. Don't even worry about anything but the two of you, got it?"

Tyler blew out a shaky breath. "Yeah. Thanks, Ez." In times like this, he was incredibly grateful for a friend like Ezra. It helped knowing someone had his back.

"Anytime." Ezra paused. "You okay?"

"Yeah. I will be." In reality, he felt wound tighter than a piano string, and his hands were shaking slightly—although that could be the need for caffeine.

"We're praying, Ty. Update us when you can."

Tyler reclined on the gurney in the small ER exam room, Murrae lying on his chest. She had fought hard against the nurse trying to insert an IV into her small hand, and Tyler had finally held her tightly against his chest to keep her from flailing as it was inserted. Now, with a tiny oxygen mask fitted over her face—which she'd allowed only him to put on—the intravenous fluids, and a full-strength fever reducer kicking in, she looked much better. He gently rubbed her back as they waited for the results of the myriad of tests the doctor had ordered.

He closed his eyes and tried to rest as well, but his brain spun out of control with thoughts and worries and scenarios. He couldn't shake this sense that something horrible was going to happen to her . . .

And he didn't think he could handle that.

He'd rather die himself than lose her. The thought made him sick to his stomach, and for a moment he thought he might heave. He laid his hand on her back and fought to find words for a prayer . . . but came up empty.

He was terrified. Terrified to death.

It wasn't like he'd even gotten a diagnosis or anything yet. And already he was terrified.

Oh, God, help me.

The four words were all he could manage as waves of memories and emotions ran over him. He practically worked in a hospital, for Pete's sake, but being here . . . again . . . with someone he loved . . . The fear was crippling.

He glanced down at Murrae and found she was asleep, looking like an angel. He gently shifted her off his chest and onto the gurney before getting to his feet. Pacing to the far side of the room, he fought to breathe normally as his heart pounded heavily, and a throb in his head matched it. Then he was breathing too fast. He gripped the counter in front of him as his head began to swirl and his chest constricted.

What . . . ?

He was having a panic attack. For the first time in his life, he was having a panic attack.

At the realization, he squeezed his eyes closed and worked to breathe slowly, in through his nose, and out through his mouth. As he concentrated on working to calm himself, he felt his chest loosening and his breathing became more even—although his hands still trembled.

Sinking into the hard plastic chair against the wall, his head dropped into his hands. He was losing it. He was well and truly losing it, and because of what?

Though he knew the fear was exaggerated, that knowledge did nothing to help.

A knock sounded, and the door opened. Tyler pushed to his feet as a young-looking man with dark hair and a white coat entered. He held out his hand, and Tyler shook it.

"Tyler? I'm Doctor Emmerson. I'm the on-call pediatrician. I spoke with the physician's assistant who examined Murrae, and I'd like to examine her myself and go over some of her test results with you."

Tyler nodded, then hesitated. *Emmerson* . . . He noted the stitched name on the doctor's coat. *Aaron J. Emmerson, MD*. "Aaron? You're Alyvia's brother, right?"

The man turned from washing his hands, then smiled. "Yes, that's correct. You two know each other?"

Tyler paused briefly. "We're . . . friends."

Was it just his imagination or did the man study him for a moment longer than normal? "Small world," he merely commented. "Now, let's take a look at the little miss." Dr. Emmerson took a seat on a rolling stool and scooted closer to the exam bed, saying hello to the now-awake Murrae and giving her an engaging smile. As he did his brief examination, he made small talk with both Murrae and Tyler. He seemed like a very nice guy—although as Alyvia's brother, Tyler would have figured as much.

As he finished making a final notation in the digital file on his iPad, he looked up at Tyler, hovering on the other side of the bed. "Why don't you sit down, Tyler, and we can talk about the test results I mentioned."

Tyler first pulled one of Murrae's books out of her bag and handed it to her before doing as the doctor suggested. He folded his hands on his knees and looked expectantly at him.

Dr. Emmerson paused only briefly before meeting Tyler's eyes. "I'll get right into it, as I believe that's what you'd prefer. Murrae is a pretty sick little lady at the moment."

Tyler exhaled slowly and had to consciously relax his hands.

"The tests we did show RSV is the virus we're looking at. Are you familiar with it?"

Tyler nodded. "Yes." He'd encountered a few cases of it over the past winter.

"As I'm sure you're aware, in certain patients, RSV can develop into pneumonia—"

"Pneumonia?" Tyler's heart dropped. Pneumonia was not good. Pneumonia was very *bad*.

Dr. Emmerson nodded. "That's what we're seeing on her chest x-ray." He looked down and swiped a few times on his iPad before handing it to Tyler.

Tyler carefully studied the digital image of the x-ray before handing it back.

"When you came in, her oxygen saturation was very low. It's still only at ninety-one percent right now, obviously still lower than I'd like it, which is why I'd like to admit her. I want to get her on an antibiotic to deal with the pneumonia and keep her on the oxygen until her sat levels stabilize. She was born prematurely?"

Tyler nodded. "She was born at thirty weeks."

"Any lung issues?"

"Not since the NICU."

The man gave a firm nod and made a notation of something on his tablet. "Okay. I think the infection just got to be more than she could handle. She's on the small side for her age, her lungs may not be quite as sound as a full term baby's, so she probably just didn't have the energy to fight this off by herself. Once those antibiotics start doing their job and her oxygen levels normalize, I think we should see her perking up pretty quickly."

"So, she'll be fine. Right?" he asked, needing the affirmation.

Dr. Emmerson hesitated for a moment, running his hand across his face. "You know I can't say that for sure. She's in pretty rough shape right now. It's possible the infection may not respond to the antibiotics. But we'll keep a close eye on her and do everything possible."

Tyler looked down at Murrae, who lay lethargically playing with the corner of the book he'd given her. She looked up at him, and his heart pinched. She looked so tired and miserable. She tugged at the oxygen mask still in place over her mouth and nose and started to cry.

"Hey, hey," he said softly, reaching out to adjust the mask, then picked her up, careful of the IV in her hand. "It's okay, pumpkin. Daddy's right here."

Dr. Emmerson reached forward and placed a pulse oximeter on her finger again, noting the reading on the digital display. Then he looked at Tyler. "We'll switch the oxygen mask for a nasal cannula once we get her in a room so she's more comfortable. Do you have any questions before I go?"

Tyler couldn't seem to think past the little girl clinging to his neck and whimpering softly, so he shook his head. "Not right now."

The doctor nodded. "Then I'll check in with you in a bit. Someone will be in shortly to get her transferred to a room."

"Thank you, Dr. Emmerson." Tyler held out his free hand and the man gave it a firm grip.

"Call me Aaron. It was good to meet you and your daughter, although I'm sorry it was in this situation. I might have to give that sister of mine a hard time about why she's never mentioned you to me," Aaron said with a wry grin that made him look far younger than he probably was.

Tyler chuckled, grabbing the lifeline of brief humor. "Please don't."

As the door closed behind the doctor, Tyler sighed, squeezing his eyes shut for a brief moment. *Pneumonia, God? Really?* That felt stupidly unfair, considering his life.

People died from pneumonia. Regularly. As a paramedic, he knew the stats of deaths from RSV and pneumonia, especially in young children.

He rubbed Murrae's back, and thankfully she seemed to be calming. Under his hand, he could feel the wheeze of her breathing in her back. If it were at all possible to transfer the sickness from her to him so she could be well, he'd do it without a second thought.

Again, he found that he didn't know what to pray. He'd prayed before in dire times, and look where it had led. Deep down, he didn't doubt that God was all powerful, or that God answered prayer. But the logical side of his brain said 800,000 children died from pneumonia each year and where was God in that?

"Why are you despairing, oh my soul? Hope in God."

The verse came unbidden to his mind, and he mentally searched for the rest of it. He must have memorized it at one time.

"Why are you despairing, oh my soul? Why are you disquieted within? Hope in God, for I shall yet praise Him; the help of my countenance, and my God."

Hope in God.

He let the words swirl around in his brain.

You can have hope.

Hope.

Tyler closed his eyes and took a deep breath. He forced all the air out, and along with it, the fear and doubt. *All right, God. This is all You. Help me to trust in You. Help me to hope in You.*

I want hope. I need *hope.*

Chapter Twenty Three

The bell above the door jingled as Alyvia stumbled down the stairs from her apartment, her hands full of boxes. When the Christmas lights—*twinkle* lights—had arrived via the big brown truck, she'd taken them upstairs to open them, but now she realized how stupid that was, as she had to bring them back *down*stairs now. Sometimes she wondered where her brain was. Although she had had a lot on her mind lately with her dad . . .

She huffed out a breath as she dropped the boxes out of sight at the bottom of the stairwell. She'd take care of them later. Looking up, she spotted who had entered the store.

Speaking of . . . She pulled out a smile as she stepped out into the main area of the store, tucking her hands into her skinny-jeans pockets. "Hey, Dad." The last word still felt awkward as it slipped off her tongue.

He turned and smiled back, causing lines to crinkle around his eyes. "Hi, Alyvia." He nervously tucked his hands in his pockets, unconsciously mirroring her posture.

She had to hide her smile and pulled her own hands out of her pockets. Apparently that was a nervous habit she had gotten from him.

"I . . . I finished the book I was reading, and thought I'd come by and see if you had something else." He still spoke tentatively, like he was talking to a stranger. It was still weird to see. She remembered her dad being bold, strong, and assertive. Not shy, tentative, and careful.

She was struck again by how she wasn't the only one changed by time and situation.

"Well, I do own a bookstore, so I'm sure I could find something," she said with a teasing grin, waving her arm to encompass the store.

He chuckled and looked down.

"What are you in the mood to read?"

He thought for a moment, pursing his lips in a way that she'd seen Aaron do when he was thinking. "How about a simple but profound contemporary?"

She snapped her fingers and started toward the contemporary section of the fiction area. Her favorite part of running a bookstore was giving recommendations to customers. And contemporary fiction was her favorite genre, so this was an easy one. She quickly located the series she was thinking of, pulled the first book off the shelf, and turned to hand it to her father.

He took it and she watched as a slow smile spread over his face. "*At Home in Mitford.*"

"Have you read it?"

He looked at her, still smiling. "Yes. It's a favorite series of mine."

She smiled back, her shoulders releasing some tension. "Mine too."

"You have good taste." He grinned.

"I guess I had a good influence."

His smile slowly faded and he looked down, as if realizing he hadn't actually been a good influence.

She mentally smacked herself. "Do you want something different?"

"No, I think I'm due to reread this one anyway. It's been awhile."

They walked back to the counter and Alyvia rang up the book and swiped his credit card. As she did so, his eyes roamed the area, and suddenly she felt self-conscious of her space.

He met her gaze as he slipped his credit card back into his wallet. "You've really got a great thing going here, Lyvy."

Her heart warmed under the praise, despite not wanting to care what he thought.

Happy Haven Books was nearly sacred to her. It was all her hopes and dreams and ambition in one tiny store. It was an extension of herself, and maybe, just maybe, it had something to do with her father, too. As if by creating a place based around their shared love of books, maybe then he would be proud of her.

Alyvia shifted, feeling vulnerable and exposed by the realization.

In response to his statement, she started rambling about how much still needed to be done and what was still lacking. She mentioned her vision for the front window display with the Christmas lights and soaked up the way her father seemed to be interested in her ideas.

"Well, I could help you with the lights if you'd like. That way you don't have to wait for your friend to be available. If you want," Dad offered hesitantly.

Alyvia paused and considered. She had yet to text Tyler, so she didn't know when he would be able to help her. Why not let her dad help? "Like, right now?"

"Sure, if you want. My day is empty."

She smiled. "Then I'd love your help."

His answering smile lit his eyes and made her glad she'd said yes. "Put me to work, then."

For the next hour, they untangled and retangled strand upon strand of white Christmas lights. Her dad stood on a step ladder in front of the picture window and strategically screwed in cup hooks to hold the lights while Alyvia directed from below.

"No, no, wait. More to the left."

"Are you sure?"

"Mm-hm. I want them to be spaced wider apart."

He finished screwing in the cup hooks and hung the strand of lights upon them, then looked at Alyvia.

Alyvia stared at them for a moment, then held up her finger and stepped out the front door to stand on the sidewalk and peer in, arms folded. She winced. It was all wrong. Not at all what she was picturing. Through the window, Dad did a thumbs up, then a thumbs down, a questioning look on his face.

She turned and reentered, the bell jingling happily.

"Well?" he asked, still perched on the stepladder.

She folded her hands together. "I have some concerns."

He laughed. "Why does that sound incredibly diplomatic?"

"Okay, we need to start over."

Now it was his turn to wince. "Completely over?"

"I'm afraid so."

He shook his head but smiled. "All right, boss. Let's start over."

An hour later, they stood side by side on the sidewalk, looking inside. Alyvia tilted her head, taking the entire display in. *Yes.* This was what she'd imagined. It was better than she'd imagined. She turned to her dad and he looked down at her.

"Now we can turn them on," she said.

He grinned. She'd been insistent on not turning the lights on until they were entirely finished, so they would be able to see the whole display all at once.

"Well, what are we waiting for?" He put his arm around her shoulders and pulled open the door. Aside from the brief and stiff hug in the restaurant, this was the first time he'd made any physical contact. She liked that he respected her space and was giving them time to reacquaint themselves with each other. But she was glad he was becoming more comfortable around her, and she was becoming more comfortable around him, as well.

He stopped in front of the window and picked up the plug end of the light strand and the end of the extension cord that ran to the nearest outlet. "Do the honors," he said, presenting both to her.

She hesitated and looked up at him. "You do the honors. You did most of the work. I just directed."

He tilted his head and gave her a look. "This was all you, Lyvy. Plug 'em in."

Grinning, she took the two ends and plugged them together. The lights flickered for a few seconds before staying on. She dropped the cord and took a step back with a small gasp.

It was beautiful, and she was only looking at the back side of it.

Dad pulled open the door again and gestured her ahead of him. She went and stood on the sidewalk again, and he stood next to her. She put her hand over her mouth and stared.

It was beautiful.

The twinkle lights hung in a curtain, creating a backdrop. Some of her favorite and most popular books were displayed on white shelves, and potted succulents and realistic pink silk flowers were tastefully arranged to add pops of color and dimension. More tiny twinkle lights draped over areas of the shelves or wrapped around a certain book to add more light.

It was everything she'd pictured, but better.

She took it all in with awe, then looked up at her dad only to find him staring at her, a small smile on his face, his eyes gentle. "What?" she whispered.

He wrapped his arm around her shoulders in a gentle half-hug. "Good job, kiddo. I'm proud of you."

Alyvia stopped, her heart captured by his words. *I'm proud of you.* Then she looked up at him. "Why?"

He chuckled and shifted. "Why? Because you went after your dreams and you made them a reality. I know it hasn't been easy, but you stuck with it. And now look at what you've done." He motioned to the window display, and she looked at it again.

Her eyes glossed over, and she clung to his words, not wanting to let them go. *I'm proud of you.* "Thanks," she whispered.

A pedestrian walked by, causing them to move out of the way, and the moment was broken. "Well," she said. "Thank you for your help. I couldn't have done it without you."

"You're more than welcome, but you could have figured it out without me."

Tell him, a voice whispered. *Tell him now.*

But she hesitated, feeling awkward. Her dad pulled open the door again and she entered, the jingling bell startling her for once.

Tell him.

Okay, okay. She turned to face him. He stood behind her, hands tucked into his pockets, the nervousness—the vulnerability—on his face again.

"Dad, I—"

185

A strange look crossed his face. "Is that smoke?"

Alyvia turned, sniffing. Something did smell like smoke. And the air had a slightly hazy look to it. Her eyes widened. Smoke was not good.

A sudden shrieking noise assaulted her ears, scaring her, and she froze.

Her dad grabbed her shoulder and she was forced to look up at him. "Where's the electrical panel?"

Mutely, she pointed in the direction of the door to the back room.

"Unplug the lights," he shouted over the sound of the smoke alarm before jogging in the direction she'd pointed.

Startled out of the shock, she did so, then hesitated. Should she call 911? Better safe than sorry. She dialed the three digits and gave her address to the dispatcher with a description of what was happening. The dispatcher promised fire trucks were on their way, then told her to stay on the line. She did so, but tucked her phone back in her pocket. The smoke was thicker now, starting to choke her and make her eyes water. Her dad would need the fire extinguisher. She hurried to the hall closet, the smoke getting heavier, and grabbed it from its place on the wall, then entered the back room.

Her heart stopped.

The back corner where the electrical panel was housed was engulfed in flames, the wood bookshelf next to it holding overstock books now burning as well. The smoke seared her eyes and she struggled to find her father. Where was he?

"Daddy!" she screamed over the sound of the alarm and the flames. Suddenly he was right in front of her, grabbing the extinguisher and shoving her back toward the door.

"Go!" he yelled, and after one more shove in the direction of the door, he turned and started using the red canister.

Everything crystallized in a moment.

The fire had gotten too far out of hand, and the small fire extinguisher wasn't going to cut it. But that wasn't going to stop her father from trying. He was going to get himself killed.

And she hadn't told him yet.

Now gagging on the smoke, she pulled her shirt collar over her mouth and nose and went after him, grabbing his shoulder and trying to pull him away. "Daddy, stop! Stop! We need to leave!"

He turned, his face blackened by soot and eyes red, tears leaving traces down his cheeks. "Alyvia, go! I've got this! You need to get out!" He coughed, then he couldn't stop. He doubled over before collapsing to his knees, fighting to breathe. Panic choked Alyvia, or maybe it was the smoke.

"Daddy!"

He pushed at her again. "Alyvia, go!" he wheezed.

He couldn't breathe. She couldn't breathe. They needed to get out. She grabbed under his shoulder and tried to drag him but quickly stalled out.

She had to accept that *she* wasn't going to be able to help him.

She needed to find help.

Stumbling to her feet, she coughed and ran through the door. Once she was in the main area, the smoke was less. She made it to the front door where three firemen were entering. She grabbed the arm of the first one, fighting to catch her breath.

"My dad! He's back there! You need to get him! The back corner of the back room," she said, pointing.

"We'll get him, ma'am." Two of them set off in the direction she had pointed, and the third grabbed her arm and tried to push her out the door, but she fought him.

"No, my dad!"

He grabbed her shoulders as she tried to go back in. "Let us do our jobs, ma'am. We can't be rescuing two people. We'll get him. You need to wait outside."

Seeing the wisdom of his words, she stopped fighting and let herself be led to the ambulance just arriving. Her throat tickled and ached, and she fought to not cough. Her eyes were streaming and she wasn't sure if it was from the smoke or if she was crying.

Daddy. Please don't die.

Chapter Twenty-Four

Tyler watched as the nurse injected an antibiotic into Murrae's IV. They had been moved to a room, and Murrae had been sleeping off and on, her body needing the rest. They switched the oxygen mask for a nasal cannula, and she had finally stopped messing with it. Tyler had been watching the display on the pulse oximeter for the past hour, and he was relieved to see her levels had stabilized, even if they were still a bit low.

After settling in their room, Tyler finally texted Ezra and Piper with an update, then texted his parents. Piper had asked if there was anything she could do, and he'd told her he'd get back to her. His mom had immediately texted back that she was on her way. Shortly after that, another text came through asking if he wanted her to come. He chuckled slightly. He knew his mom's first instinct would be to show up immediately, but then he envisioned his dad calming her down and suggesting that maybe just showing up wouldn't actually be that helpful.

He loved his parents. He texted her back and told her to hold off for now, hoping that by tomorrow morning at the latest they would be going home anyway. As soon as the antibiotics had a chance to start their work and her breathing was normal. He glanced at his phone as it vibrated again.

We're praying, hon. Keep us updated and give her a kiss from me. Love you both.

Yeah, he loved his parents. They had been endlessly helpful and supportive during Sabrina's hospital stays and after her passing. And after Murrae was out of the NICU, they made adjusting to life with a newborn easier. Or rather as easy as it could be for a single parent.

As he started to put his phone back into his pocket, he hesitated. Should he text Alyvia? Was that . . . too much? As he'd told Aaron, they were just friends. He wryly remembered the man's face. Alyvia had at least one protective big brother. But for some reason that thought didn't deter him.

Deciding texting her would be too personal, he pushed his phone into his pocket and looked over at Murrae. He had found a cartoon on the television that had kept her occupied for the last hour, but now she was starting to fall asleep again. He turned the volume down and watched as her eyelids fluttered closed and stayed closed, her breathing evening out.

She was so perfect. With her thick, dark lashes brushing her round cheeks and curly soft hair spilling over the pillow, only the oxygen cannula stretching across her face and the IV in her hand ruined the picture. His gut clenched to see her in this atmosphere. When he'd carefully placed her tiny body in the pink and gray car seat and tucked a soft blanket around her that day she was released from the NICU, he prayed to never find himself in this place again. In a hospital. With a loved one in the bed, suffering. And himself completely and utterly incapable of doing anything about it.

He hated that helpless feeling. Never in his life had he ever been so aware of his own ineptitude as he'd stood beside Sabrina, then Murrae, both of them hooked up to machines and monitors that kept them alive. And there had been literally nothing he could do.

As the too-familiar emotion washed over him again, he brushed back the hair from Murrae's face and gently placed his palm over her forehead.

Jesus, please heal this little one. It cuts me in pieces to see her here—again. Heal her body and give her strength.

He felt the exhaustion weighing down his limbs. He hadn't slept well the past two nights. Today had been draining and it wasn't even noon yet. Assured she was sound asleep, he checked the monitors by her bedside one last time, then sank onto the pull-out couch by the window.

Within seconds, he felt himself drifting.

A harsh beeping penetrated his consciousness sometime later, and he forced himself to wake up. He cracked his eyes open and glanced around the room, orienting himself. Then he swung his legs down and shot to his feet in one swift move, hurrying the few steps to the bedside.

Murrae blinked up at him, pure terror in her wide blue eyes as they locked onto his. It took only a glance to determine the cause of the machine's alarm. Murrae's lips were blue and she was gasping, fighting to breathe. Her pale skin was flushed, and red hives had broken out on her neck.

Tyler felt his own panic ballooning even as he fought for clarity on what to do. But before he could even do anything, a nurse rushed into the room, quickly followed by more medical personnel. A doctor started barking out orders.

"Point oh-one milligrams of Epi IM! Let's get a large-bore line in her ASAP with twenty mil of normal saline. I want to be ready to intubate if needed."

Tyler stumbled backward as everyone worked in a flurry of movement. Once again, he felt suffocated by that feeling of helplessness. He had the knowledge and the skills to know what to do, but he didn't have the necessary tools. Or calm. He was completely useless as his daughter fought for her life.

Look at Me.

He breathed. In. Out. *Jesus.*

Look at Me. I'm fighting for you.

Another breath. *Jesus. Jesus, Jesus, Jesus.* It was all he could do.

He was able to see Murrae's face through the whirl of medical personnel, and he found her looking at him. Her bright blue eyes stared at him, the fear in them torturing him. He wanted nothing more than to hold her close and let her know it was all going to be okay. *Jesus, hold her.*

I am.

Unable to look away and not wanting to, they stared at each other. And he saw the terror in her eyes dissipate as she calmed, despite the chaos of the medical staff around her.

She trusted him.

Finally, everything calmed down. The doctor looked up and addressed him. "She's stable now."

Tyler blew out a breath and was by her side in an instant, brushing her hair from her face, kissing her forehead and telling her how brave she was. He heard Aaron hustle in behind him.

"I just got paged."

"She's stabilized," the other doctor addressed Aaron. Tyler overheard them conferring but was too focused on Murrae to pay any attention.

Still holding Murrae's hand, he turned toward the doctors and gave them his attention.

The doctor—he squinted at the embroidered name on his white coat—Dennis Mason, addressed him first. "Murrae had an allergic reaction and went into anaphylactic shock."

Tyler nodded, knowing that already.

"Does she have any known allergies?"

Tyler shook his head. "No."

"Has she ever previously been prescribed an antibiotic, particularly the one she was put on today?" he asked, naming the drug.

"No. Was it the antibiotic that she reacted to?"

"If I had to guess, that's what mine would be. It's possible for patients to have an allergic reaction to certain antibiotics. That would have been the only out-of-the-norm thing she was exposed to."

"So now what?" Tyler asked.

Dr. Mason deferred to Aaron as the pediatrician and Murrae's doctor. "We'll change her prescription to a different antibiotic, and we'll also keep a close eye on her to watch for a biphasic reaction—a recurrence of the symptoms. She's on a small dose of epinephrine for now to help with the hypotension. She'll probably be sleepy for a bit from the epi, but like I said, she'll be closely monitored."

Tyler nodded and blew out a shaky breath, some of the tension lessening for the first time since he'd been awakened. He looked down at Murrae, who was snuggled up next to his arm, starting to look drowsy as Aaron had said. Tyler reached over and shook Dr. Mason's hand. "Thank you," he said, meeting the man's green eyes.

He nodded, then left.

Aaron tucked his hands into the pockets of his white coat and sank onto the rolling stool on the opposite side of the bed. He watched Murrae for a moment before playfully tapping her nose, eliciting a tiny smile even as she drew closer to Tyler. "She's a tough kid."

Tyler nodded, looking down at her. She peered up at him, then her tiny finger reached up and poked his lips. "'Appy," her small voice rasped.

He couldn't not smile. "She is a fighter."

"I'm sorry, Tyler. This was just bad luck. We're doing everything we can to get Miss Murrae feeling like herself again."

Tyler nodded and looked up at Aaron as he pushed to his feet. "Thank you." He cleared the emotion from his throat.

He felt like he was barely hanging on by a thread.

Aaron clapped him on the shoulder as he turned. "Hang tough."

Yup. He was hanging.

He held Murrae's hand and stroked her hair until she dozed off. Then he pushed to his feet and stepped into the hallway, glancing left and right before spotting an empty family room almost directly across from Murrae's room. He didn't want to be any great distance from her.

Entering, he made his way to the window on the far side of the room. It gave a second story view of a residential area adjacent to the hospital. He braced his hand against the window frame and let the wall take his weight as he stared out the window, unseeing.

Emotion—all the fear, grief, anger he'd felt in the last two days and the past few years—clogged his throat, and he fought for control. Fought to hold himself together. Fought the jagged pieces of himself—a man he hardly recognized anymore—that wanted to fly apart.

Sinking into a chair, he leaned forward, his elbows braced on his knees and his fist pressing against his mouth.

Let go. I can hold you, too, if you'll let Me.

He was unable to hold back the sobs.

Chapter Twenty-Five

Alyvia stood outside the exam room her father had disappeared into what seemed like ages ago. He hadn't really been conscious on the short ambulance ride to the ER. She, on the other hand, had been examined and discharged with a prescription for an inhaler to manage the cough and ache in her lungs, but she had no other injuries.

She was grateful for that, but all she wanted was to see her dad. They'd asked her to wait for now. She had taken the time to text her mom and siblings about the ordeal, and couldn't help envisioning a horde of Emmersons descending upon the hospital en masse. Her mom said she would meet her at the hospital as soon as she could leave work, and her siblings who had responded had asked for timely updates.

"Lyv!"

She turned to find Aaron jogging down the hallway toward her. He pulled to a stop in front of her and seemed to visually sweep her for injuries before smushing her face between his hands and scrutinizing her carefully. "I just saw your text. Are you okay? Did you get checked out? What did the doctor say? Who examined you? Are you okay?"

She tugged at his hands to loosen his hold. "Aaron, stop. I'm fine."

He dropped his hands to her shoulders, still searching her face. "Are you sure?"

"Yes." Her untimely cough seemed to bely her words, and her brother's face grew concerned. "Just a cough, and my chest aches a little bit. That's it. I promise."

His concern allayed, he pulled her into a tight hug. "Good. Good." He paused and she clung to the hug, grateful for the solidarity of it at the moment. "Now don't ever text me like that again, all right? I'd much rather get a call. Actually, just don't find yourself here again at all, okay?"

She smiled faintly against his pale green button-up. "'Kay." Then she pulled back. "Dad. They won't let me see him." Her face crumpled and she found herself crying—again. "Aaron, I didn't get to tell him. I waited too long. What if it's too late?"

"Shh, it's not too late," he said, pulling her back into a hug. "What were you going to tell him?"

She sniffled and whispered, "I needed to tell him I forgive him. And I wanted to say that I was sorry."

He just held her for a moment. When he did speak, she could sense the emotion hovering in his voice. "It's not too late, Lyv. He's going to be okay."

She could only hope he was right. "I . . . I want to be a family again," she said, holding in a sob.

His arms tightened around her, and his voice was hoarse. "Me too, Lyv. Me too."

A doctor finally stepped out of the exam room and Aaron shifted them to face the woman, his arm still slung around Alyvia's shoulders.

"Rachel, how is he?"

She looked at him. "Your father, right?"

Aaron nodded. "This is my sister, Alyvia."

The doctor gave Alyvia a nod in greeting and addressed them both. "He's fine."

Relief washed over Alyvia in what felt like a literal wave. She felt the tension drain out of Aaron as well.

Thank you, Jesus. He's going to be okay!

Tell him now.

She would this time. Just as soon as she could get in there.

"He inhaled a lot of smoke and was unconscious when he was brought in, which is a concern, but he seems to be doing better now. He's refusing to be admitted, but I'm going to keep him on oxygen and a bronchodilator for a bit. I'm also prescribing an antibiotic just to be safe."

Aaron started to ask a question, but Alyvia had heard all she needed to. She tapped his arm to interrupt him and asked the doctor, "Can I see him?"

"Of course," she said kindly, shifting away from the door.

Alyvia looked up at Aaron.

He gave her a smile and nudged her away. "Go."

She opened the door and quietly stepped into the room, closing the door part way behind her. The lights had been dimmed slightly, and a soft beeping noise emitted from a machine she guessed was monitoring his heart rate. Her dad lay with his eyes closed, and she wondered if he was asleep. An oxygen mask was on his face, an IV in his arm, and a blood pressure cuff around his bicep. He was still in the clothes he had been wearing, although they were tattered now.

She stopped beside the bed and hesitated. His eyes opened and immediately found her face. Tears welled in his already reddened eyes and spilled down his temples. He reached out his hand toward her while pushing aside the mask with his other. "You're okay?" His voice was hoarse, much worse than hers, and she winced.

She gripped his hand in both of hers. "Yes, I'm okay."

He searched her face. "Good, good." The word rasped and he turned away as he fought to muffle a painful sounding cough. He leaned back again, breathless.

She squeezed his hand, her heart aching that he was hurt, because of her.

"Daddy, please put the mask back on." Her insistent tone had him glancing at her before he reached to put the mask back over his mouth and nose. Satisfied, she drew a deep breath, then regretted it as it tickled her aching throat. She swallowed carefully to avoid breaking into a coughing fit. They were quite a pair.

"Daddy, listen. I want to tell you something."

His eyes roamed her face, looking confused.

"I want you to know . . . I need to say, I forgive you." The words sounded stark once she said them, but as she watched, his face crumpled and more tears leaked out. His emotion wrecked her careful composure, and she struggled not to cry again. She pulled a tissue out of the box on the wall and gently dabbed at the sides of his face as she searched for words to continue. *Jesus, help me.*

She forced herself to meet his eyes. "And I need to say I'm sorry."

He instantly started to shake his head, and she shook hers back and held up a hand.

"No, please, just listen."

He nodded, and she continued.

I need to say I'm sorry for being so angry with you. I held onto my bitterness because I thought it would keep me safe from being hurt again. But all it did was hurt me more, and it hurt you and Mom, and the others. And I'm sorry I was too bitter to see how you were hurting, too. I'm so sorry, Daddy. I don't want to be mad anymore." She bit her lip as she struggled not to cry, but it didn't seem she had a say in the matter. The tears fell down her cheeks anyway, choking her throat from saying any more even if she had wanted to.

Her dad had his fingers pressing against his eyelids, his face tight as his body shook slightly with emotion. Alyvia didn't know whether she should leave or stay or . . . what? She wanted to find a private room and bawl her eyes out.

Then her father held out his arms to her, tears still trickling down his face. The look of love and understanding and . . . acceptance in his eyes made her hesitate. Then she leaned against the edge of the bed and fell into him, his arms folding around her securely, his hand stroking her hair, his chest heaving beneath her. They were weeping together, but the release was cathartic—healing, not painful.

After a few moments, he spoke, his voice rasping and rumbling in his chest beneath her ear. "I love you, Alyvia Faye. That's what I need you to know. I love you."

She used the back of her hand to wipe the wetness from her face, then closed her eyes and hugged him tighter. "I love you, too, Daddy."

Alyvia's mom, Micah, and Piper were in the hall when Alyvia finally stepped from the room. Man, she was starting to feel smothered. She assured everyone she was okay, that Dad was okay, and received hugs all around. She joked that she ought to end up in the ER more often if it was what she had to do to get more hugs. Micah glared at her with a *don't-you-dare* look, and Aaron playfully smacked her on the back of the head.

Piper tugged her aside as her mom went in to see her dad and her brothers drifted off in conversation. They slipped into a small alcove in the hallway with chairs, and Piper made her sit in one. "You look tired."

Alyvia smiled faintly, feeling that. "That's probably the nicest way to say how I look right now."

Piper just leaned closer and slid her arm through Alyvia's, rubbing it. "How are you, really?"

Alyvia took a deep breath, grateful for the comfort and understanding of a friend at a time when she felt so vulnerable. "I'm . . . I'm good. Actually." And she was. She felt good. She told her friend about what had happened between her and her father. Afterward, they sat in silence for a few moments, and Alyvia felt the exhaustion lapping over her.

"I'm proud of you, you know," Piper said softly. "It takes a lot of guts to forgive and to ask for forgiveness."

Alyvia wouldn't be rid of the ache of regret for a long time when she thought of how she'd almost been too late. "It took me forever, though."

"But you did it." Piper squeezed her arm. Piper had never been close with either of her parents, and Alyvia knew it was something she still struggled with.

Alyvia squeezed back. "Thank you for coming. You didn't have to."

"As if you could stop me."

Alyvia smiled. Loyalty ran deep and strong in her friend. "Who's with the kids?"

"Tom's watching them for a few hours, the saint," she said with affection. While she may not be in touch with her parents, the bond between Piper and her father-in-law was a sweet one. "It's not often more than one of my friends ends up here, and I can't say I like it," she continued with a shake of her head.

More than one . . . "What? Who else is here?"

Piper leaned forward to look at her, an odd look on her face. "You didn't know? Tyler's here."

Apprehension and worry bubbled up in her chest and she tried to keep hold of it. "What? Why? Is he okay?"

Piper shook her head. "It's Murrae. She's been sick for a few days, and when she started to have some breathing issues, he wanted to get her checked out. Whatever she had morphed into pneumonia. Tyler said they wanted to keep her here until her oxygen levels were okay."

Alyvia's heart sank like lead. It made her sad to think about such a tiny, sweet thing like Murrae being sick and hospitalized. "Oh no. The poor thing. Is she doing all right?"

Piper shrugged. "Last I heard. I was going to go check up on them after I found you."

Poor Tyler. Her heart ached for the two of them. The duo had been through so much already. She wondered how he was handling it. She wanted to go find him. Talk to him. See what she could do to help. Suddenly, her exhaustion and other worries were pushed to the side, and she found herself wanting to do what she could to make things easier for him.

And Murrae, she told herself. *This is about Murrae.* Not for the first time she found herself wondering if she had formed an unhealthy attachment to the two. She liked them—a lot.

She liked *him*.

Piper was studying her face, an indecipherable look on her own face. It was half-smirk, half something else.

"What?" Alyvia asked.

"Nothing."

"No, what? You're making a weird face."

Yes, that was definitely a smirk. "*You're* the one making a funny face. You like him, don't you?"

Alyvia frowned at her friend. She didn't realize she was so transparent. She felt heat creeping into her cheeks the longer her friend stared at her. "It's a horrible idea, isn't it?"

Piper shook her head, still smiling. "Of course it's not." Piper leaned closer to whisper conspiratorially. "Because he likes *you*."

Alyvia leaned back, eyes wide. Then they narrowed. "How do you know?"

"Ez says so, and I see it too."

"How does he know?" Guys weren't that observant about these things . . . were they? Although if anyone was, it was Ezra.

Giving Alyvia an annoyed look, Piper gave her head a slight shake. "He's not blind, or deaf, silly. Tyler mentions you *all* the time. And who just ignores their busy life to help a 'friend,'" Piper used her fingers to make air quotes, "fix up their bookstore?"

"He didn't . . ." Alyvia faintly protested, trailing off as Piper yet again shook her head.

"I'm not making this stuff up, Lyv."

Alyvia let the realization roll around in her head. But . . . "Piper, he lost his *wife*."

"Yes, he did. Nearly two years ago. I'm not saying there's a timetable on grief—I know that well—but while his head may not have caught up yet, his heart is healing. I'm not saying he should or would get married tomorrow—"

Alyvia swallowed hard at the thought.

"But he's ready to move on. If I know him at all, I think that much is true."

Alyvia rubbed her arms, staring at the tile floor. This was so much more complicated than she had ever imagined. As a little girl, she'd imagined falling in love was so simple and lovely. She mentally choked. Not that anyone was falling in love . . . yet.

"Not to change the subject, as this one is very interesting . . ."

It was Alyvia's turn to give Piper a look. "Please don't tease me. At least not right now."

Piper's teasing grin turned to a gentle smile. "Of course. So, the bookstore . . . ?"

Alyvia grimaced. She'd been avoiding thinking about it. She was afraid of how much damage she might find, and was afraid of the major headache—that was probably an understatement—getting it all sorted out was going to be. Her dream . . . She wanted to rush there and see how bad it was, but at the same time didn't want to know. "I've been trying not to think about it."

"I'm sorry, Lyv." Piper's hand rubbed her back. She had the comforting "mom touch" down. "You'll have help sorting everything out. I promise. Do you know how it started?"

"Thanks. I'm pretty sure it was from the electrical. The fire started in the back room where the electrical panel is. Dad and I had just plugged in all the Christmas lights . . ." Her voice trailed off, remembering. "They were really pretty, but they probably all exploded now."

"We'll get it fixed just like it was," Piper said.

Alyvia nodded and tried to force herself not to think about it right now. That overwhelming feeling washed over her when she did, and she didn't think she had the mental stamina to process it right now.

She was exhausted. Mentally, physically, emotionally.

Piper's phone rang just then and she checked it. "It's Ez, probably checking in. I'll be a few minutes. Tyler and Murrae are on the second floor," Piper said matter-of-factly, giving the room number.

Alyvia gave her a look, but Piper just raised her brows and shrugged as she answered the phone, mouthing *Go* when Alyvia didn't move.

Fine. She did want to see him—and Murrae—but she didn't want Piper to know how eager she was to do so.

She found the elevator and took it to the second floor of the small hospital, trying to orient herself and find the proper room number amidst the confusing hallways. She was horrible at navigating places like this. Finally, she found the hallway with the proper range of room numbers listed. She started down it, glancing around. She passed an empty waiting room on her left, then paused and took two steps back. Not empty.

Tyler sat hunched over in one of the chairs, his back to her. She stepped into the room, then stopped, wondering if she should disturb him . . . She hesitated for a few seconds and was about to turn when he suddenly shoved himself to his feet and turned toward her, startling her.

He seemed just as surprised to see her. They simply stared at each other for a second, and she couldn't help but notice how haggard he looked. She was pretty sure she didn't look fabulous either, but . . . His face was drawn and tense and he looked like he might have a headache. And his face was red and blotchy, as if he had been . . . crying.

She swallowed, feeling awkward. "Hey." She smiled. "Piper said you were here. I just wanted . . ." What *did* she want? "To see if there was anything I could do for you guys."

He nodded, but his face didn't move from its serious lines. "Thanks. I was just headed back to Murrae's room." He gestured past her and walked to the door. He didn't smile. Or grin that trademark grin of his.

It was weird to see him so serious. He always seemed to handle everything with humor and grace. Nothing fazed him. It was something she admired about him.

But right now, he was fazed.

She followed him, jumping on the safer topic. "How is she doing?" *How are you doing?*

"She's doing okay right now," he said as he entered the room.

The light in the room was dimmed slightly, and Alyvia's eyes immediately sought out the bed. Looking dwarfed by her surroundings, Murrae lay curled on her side on the bed, her hands tucked beneath her face. She slept peacefully, her breathing making a slight wheezing sound. An oxygen cannula wrapped around her cheeks under her nose, and Alyvia spotted the tape covering nearly her whole hand, holding an IV in place. Another IV was in her other arm.

The poor, sweet thing.

She was aware of Tyler sinking into the chair next to the bedside and slouching down into it, as if that short walk across the hallway had been exhausting. Spotting a stool on wheels on the opposite side of the bed, she moved toward it and sat down. She sent him a glance and found him looking at Murrae.

"How are *you*?" she asked softly.

She felt him look over at her, but now she was looking at Murrae. Seemed safer than making eye contact . . .

"I'm good," he said finally.

Now she did look up at him. She forced a gentle teasing tone with a smile. "C'mon, Tyler. Friends don't lie to each other."

He frowned at her. Then looked back at the bed. "Well, I'm not the one in a hospital bed, so there's that."

She was quiet for a moment. *God, he's hurting. What do I even say to him?* She didn't want to just leave him, alone. "She's going to be okay, Ty."

He looked at her, and she was surprised at the sharpness in his face. "You don't know that."

She blinked. He was *angry*. And he was right—she didn't know that. But at the same time . . . she did. "Tyler . . . she is. Everyone's praying for her. She's getting the medical help she needs. She'll be fine. She's tough. You have to believe that."

He leaned forward, and while he kept the volume of his voice down to not wake Murrae, she could hear the harshness behind it anyway. "She already almost died. She nearly *died*, Alyvia."

Alyvia straightened, staring at him. "What . . . what do you mean?"

"She had an allergic reaction to the antibiotic and went into anaphylactic shock. She couldn't breathe. She just looked at me, terrified and having no idea what was going on . . . and I couldn't do anything." His voice hoarsened at the end and he pushed to his feet and paced to the other end of the room.

No wonder. She glanced at Murrae again. The sweet girl. She *was* tough. "I . . . I'm sorry, Tyler. I know how you must have felt . . ."

He spun back around. "But that's the thing, Alyvia. You don't know. You can't know. You have no idea what any of this is like!" His voice hissed across the room.

Alyvia felt like she had been slapped. She blinked. Standing, she searched for words—and calm. "That's not a fair statement. You're not the only one who has ever felt fear or grief or . . . or pain. No, I haven't lost a spouse—" He seemed to flinch at the reminder and she almost regretted it. "But I have felt my share of pain, just like everyone else in this world. So if you think you're alone, you're dead wrong."

He folded his arms and turned away from her again. "You know, I'm not really in the mood for company—or a sermon—right now."

Sure, she'd go. But she wasn't finished yet. "I'll gladly leave you to wallow in your self-pity if you'd like. I may not know much, but I do know this: You can't save the world, Tyler. You were never created to, and you're gonna fail every time you try. Because only one Person can do that job. And He never fails."

She waited a few moments, but he didn't say anything or turn around. His shoulders stayed in a stiff, straight line. Feeling on the verge of crumbling, she turned toward the door. She paused, glancing back at him, then shook her head.

She made it past a few more doors down the hallway before stopping and leaning against the wall, fighting tears.

His rejection ached and twisted a painful spot.

She wanted to be mad at him, but mostly she just felt . . . hurt. Sad. For him. He was hurting, but he wouldn't let anyone in.

At least, not her.

Lord Jesus, this hurts. Help him. Heal his heart. Help him to forgive himself. Show him how much you love him.

Well, she could pray for him, at least. He couldn't stop her from doing that.

Chapter Twenty-Six

Tyler didn't move for several long seconds. Then he sank onto the couch by the window, cupping his forehead in his palm.

He'd made a mess of everything.

He *was* a mess.

And Alyvia wasn't wrong. In fact, she was so right, the words struck a chord deep inside him and twisted and ached. And he had become angry and defensive.

In the turmoil of the past three years, he'd coped in the only way he could: doing. After Sabrina's diagnosis, he'd researched to death those horrible two words: glioblastoma multiforme. Then he'd made appointments with nearly every single specialist in the entire state of Washington. He worked and researched and did everything he could think to do. Now he could see that the extreme mental and physical exhaustion that had nearly incapacitated him after Sabrina's death was more than just grief. He'd given all the strength he had and all the strength she didn't have into the fight.

And with Murrae, it was now second nature to do everything he could to keep her from everything unknown. After she came home from the NICU, he spent too many nights to count in the chair by her crib, watching her sleep, making sure she didn't stop breathing. He had become the epitome of a helicopter parent without even trying.

He did everything he could physically do to keep those he loved safe and well, and Alyvia was right. He failed. Every. Single. Time. Because he left out the most important part of the equation—faith.

Even trusting God was too scary, so he gave it lip service—of course he trusted God—and left even Him out of it.

The realization struck him like a blow, and he groaned.

"Oh God, I'm so sorry. I'm so sorry," he whispered.

In holding on so tightly, he only found himself losing everything.

"Help me trust You. Alyvia is right. I wasn't made to do this. I know You're strong enough for the both of us. Help me believe it." He squeezed his eyes shut and drew a deep breath that left his body in a shudder. Tension still wound across his shoulders and up his neck. He tilted his head left and right in an effort to loosen it.

I'm letting go, Jesus. For real this time.

For real. He was done trying to do this on his own. He was done *doing*.

"Knock knock?"

He straightened and looked toward the doorway. Piper stood there, concern forming a wrinkle on her brow. They were the same age, and while he looked a lot worse for the wear, she didn't seem old enough to be the mother of two. Although she had changed a lot from the young woman he had first met with a bullet hole in one shoulder and a load of emotional baggage on the other. And had somehow managed to steal his best friend's heart in the process.

"Hey, Piper. Come on in."

"I didn't want to interrupt you. You looked lost in thought."

He shook his head and stood. "You didn't. And you didn't have to come up. I'd hate for you to bring any germs home to the kids."

She smiled at him. "I'll be careful. And I wanted to. I figured you might like some company, and Ezra's working, obviously. Besides, I wanted to see Alyvia too."

Tyler gave her a confused look. "Cascade Valley Hospital was the best place you could come up with to meet? There are such things as coffee shops, you know."

Piper frowned and stared at him for a brief second. "But Alyvia was already here . . ."

He froze. "She was?"

Piper shook her head. "I assumed she told you. There was a fire at the bookstore. She and her dad were brought in. Although they're both fine and won't be admitted," she hurried to say as she caught the expression on his face.

He stared at her, wide-eyed. Then turned and paced away a few steps with a groan, covering his face with his hands as shame washed over him anew. "I am a major, regular, class-A jerk."

There was a beat of silence, then, "Tyler. What did you do?" He could hear Piper's mama bear side emerging in her tone.

He turned back toward her, tucking his hands in his pockets and staring at her Keds tennis shoes. "I . . . was a jerk."

"Yeah, you said that. Specifically?"

He winced. "I was . . . angry. I snapped, and she said some things that were . . . entirely true, but made me defensive." He looked at her, then winced again. "Please don't look at me like that. I feel awful about it, and now I feel even worse." A band of pressure tightened across his forehead, increasing the dull throb.

Piper sighed and shook her head, moving to sit in the chair. Then she looked up at him. "It's not like you to be angry, Ty."

He rubbed his temples. "I know."

Studying him, she asked softly, "Are you okay?"

He thought for a moment before answering. "I'm getting there." He gave her a small smile, rubbing his forehead again with his fingertips. "Being here . . . it's brought back memories. But maybe I needed the slap in the face to realize a few things."

She nodded slowly. "I can understand that. We've been praying for you both."

"I know. And I appreciate it."

They were both quiet for a few minutes before Piper said, "You know, we probably ought to stop spending time in hospitals together."

He laughed, finally feeling able to see some humor. "Tell me about it." Piper and Ezra had spent many hours in waiting rooms, keeping him company or just being there during Sabrina's many hospital visits. And he knew Piper was thinking of the time her then-fiancé spent five days in a coma. They had passed a fair amount of time together then too.

Piper asked about Murrae, and Tyler told her what had happened and how she was doing.

"I'm sorry, Ty. That's a rough day," she said sympathetically, smiling wryly at her understatement.

"Something like that."

She stood and silently wrapped her arms around his waist, pulling him into a comforting hug. Ezra was the brother he never had, and over time Piper had grown nearly as close. He appreciated her quiet sympathy.

"It's going to be okay, Ty. It is."

"I know."

And he did. Now. Because it wasn't on his shoulders anymore, and the relief was immense. He could physically feel the tension draining out of his back, leaving him exhausted but peaceful.

It was all going to be okay.

Right after he made some apologies.

Chapter Twenty-Seven

A lyvia slipped her key into the lock on the front door of Happy Haven Books. The store was dark and empty inside, and she already missed the cheery welcome of the window display she and her father had created. She pushed the door open, steeling herself for what she might find. The bell above the door rang out and some of the tension faded at the familiar sound.

She paused just inside the door. It had been three whole days since the fire. Since those moments with her father she never wanted to forget. Since that encounter with Tyler she wished she *could* forget. She hadn't heard from him since, and while she told herself that he was probably very busy and tired, his words still stuck in her mind and stung.

She hadn't realized how much she had come to rely on him as a good friend until he'd pushed her away. She didn't know if they would ever again have the friendship they'd had—or anything more. His rejection felt all too similar to her father's, and she had been fighting the spiral of rejection and bitterness that threatened to tear at her self-confidence yet again. She found herself wondering if his rejection had to do with . . . her.

Shaking her head as if to shake the thought away, she looked around the place. It seemed mostly undisturbed, but the smell of smoke hung heavy in the air. She wrinkled her nose. As she walked closer to the back room, a fine layer of soot coated everything. Where to even start? The back room was completely trashed. Thankfully her stock had been mostly shelved, so while there weren't many books in the room, what was there would all need to be thrown away.

The fire marshal had done his inspection and concluded that there was only cosmetic damage, although nearly all of the electrical would need to be redone. It was her Christmas lights that sparked the fire, he had said. It was just too much for the electrical panel.

Alyvia sighed and tried not to cry as she stared at the melted, blackened mess. Despair crashed over her. Her dream . . . nearly taken out in one fell swoop. She supposed she should be grateful that it wasn't any worse, but . . . With all the work she had already put into the store, this was overwhelming.

Determined not to wallow in self-pity—though she was strongly tempted—she found a notepad and started making notes of things that needed to be done and numbering them in order of priority. Calling her insurance company to figure out the next steps was at the top of the list. She took a deep breath, then coughed as the acrid air filled her already sensitive lungs. She mentally rearranged her priorities. Number one: air the place out.

She propped the front door open and the fresh, warm May air wafted in, refreshing her. Then she took the stairs to her upper apartment two at a time and came back with a fan. She needed more than one, but this would get things started for today. She propped it on a ledge by the door to blow the smoky air out and plugged it in. *Snap.* She didn't have electricity. Groaning, she set the useless fan back on the floor and tiredly rubbed her face.

It seemed she wasn't going to be as productive today as she had wanted. All she really wanted to do was be alone and tune out the world with a good book for a few hours. But she'd call the insurance company first so she could at least say she'd done *something* today.

Alyvia tucked her notepad back into her backpack and made her way to the fiction section to find a new book that would keep her interest. She settled on a Dee Henderson romantic suspense novel she hadn't read yet. It was about Navy SEALs and sounded intriguing—and enough to keep her mind busy, anyway.

After writing a sticky note on the front counter to remind herself that she'd taken the book off the shelves, she climbed the stairs to her apartment. Thankfully, aside from a faint smoke smell that had drifted up—and the lack of electricity—it was undamaged. She was staying with her mom until she could get the electricity situation sorted out, but right now she'd rather be alone in her own space than go back to her mom's house.

Funny how in just a few short weeks, "home" had switched from the house she'd grown up in to her apartment.

After spending a solid forty-five minutes on the phone with an insurance representative, she sighed deeply and settled on her bed under a cozy-soft plush blanket and opened her book. But her eyes didn't take in the words.

She sighed. There was nothing more she could do about the things that wouldn't leave her mind, and it was driving her crazy. She squeezed her eyes closed as her mind formed a prayer.

Jesus, I give it all to you. The worry, the hurt . . . You can handle it better than I can. Thank you that I don't have to carry it.

She had to force her mind to stop spinning everything in circles. And once she started reading, she was sucked into the story as a lifeguard—the protagonist—attempted to rescue a boy in the frigid ocean as night set in. Pages flew by until she was startled out of the fictional world and back into the real one by a loud knock on her apartment door.

She set her book down and tossed the blanket aside. Wonder of wonders, she had actually been able to forget about reality for—she checked the time—nearly two hours. She hurried to the door, confused as to who would be knocking. Pulling it open, her eyes widened in surprise. Tall, blond, and blue-eyed as ever, Tyler stood on the other side, hand raised as if he was going to knock again.

Neither of them spoke for a moment. *He is really quite good-looking.* Instantly, Alyvia mentally face-palmed herself for the thought. But with those bright blue eyes, strong cheekbones and jaw, and a cleft in his chin that made most girls swoon . . . he *was*. New stress lines seemed to have appeared around his eyes and between his brows, and he looked tired, but . . . peaceful. Not at all tense and angsty like he had been at the hospital.

His hand slowly lowered back to his side, then he smiled. "Hi."

Alyvia found herself smiling back. "Hey. How's it going?"

"I knocked three times and was starting to wonder if you were here. But the front door was open."

She frowned. "Oh. Sorry, I didn't even hear it until the last time. I was reading," she said, as if that explained it.

Tyler grinned, looking like he was going to tease her about it. Then the grin faded as he shifted and ran his palm across the back of his neck. He pointed back down the stairs. "Want to take a walk? It's a nice day out."

She thought for a moment, then simply said, "Okay." Stepping forward, she closed the door behind her. Tyler shifted to the side of the landing to let her go down the stairs first. He silently followed her down and through the store, pausing and peering in as they passed the door to the back room. She hesitated as she reached the front, waiting on him. His expression was unreadable as he stared around for a few seconds then followed her.

Well, he was strangely quiet. Usually he didn't shut up—and she meant that in the nicest way possible. It was just *him*.

Alyvia locked the front door behind them and they started off down the sidewalk, side-by-side. Tyler tucked his hands in the pockets of his dark-wash jeans. Alyvia unconsciously put her hands in her jeans pockets, then pulled them back out.

Several paces down the sidewalk, Tyler finally sent a side-glance at her and spoke, his tone serious and genuine. "I'm really sorry about Happy Haven. That really stinks."

"Thank you," she said softly. "And it does. Quite literally," she added, smiling at her own jest.

He chuckled quietly, then sobered, squinting upward. "I didn't know . . ." he trailed off. *When I yelled at you,* seemed to hang in the air, unspoken but implied. "How's your dad?" He sidestepped to allow another pedestrian to pass, his arm bumping her shoulder. Given the foot in height difference, they probably stood out walking together.

"He's doing well. Taking it easy. He still sounds pretty hoarse and has an inhaler for the coughing, but his doctor said he'll be completely normal in a few more days."

He bobbed his head. "Good. That's good." Then he glanced at her again. "And you?"

She gave him a small smile. "I'm good too."

He studied her more closely. "No shortness of breath? Confusion? Bad cough?"

Shaking her head, she forced herself not to smile and took a deep breath to demonstrate. Just a tiny twinge in her chest. "Nothing worth noting. Promise. Are you a medical professional or something?" she teased.

He grinned. "Something like that."

The tension seemed to ease, and she was glad. They walked on for a few more blocks, talking about Murrae—she was much better and home with Ellen right now—and he asked more about the bookstore. As they walked, they reached Arlington Park on the edge of the Stillaguamish River, the town's northernmost border. The park was one of Alyvia's favorite places with its gorgeous views of the river, and she was glad they had ended up here. Finally, Tyler stopped and turned toward her as they reached a lookout point over the river. His face grew serious again.

"Alyvia, I owe you an apology," he started.

Now she did tuck her hands in her pockets, shaking her head. "No, it's fi—"

Tyler shook his head too, holding up a hand. "No, I do. I was . . . horrible to you."

"It was a really bad day, for both of us," she said with a shrug. "I was probably out of line too." Alyvia hated conflict and wished they could simply move on.

"No. You were right, which is why I got so upset. And yes, it was a bad day, but that's not an excuse for my words or actions." His hand reached out and touched her arm, then dropped. She looked up at him and met his gaze—steady and full of remorse. He took a deep breath. "Alyvia, I'm really sorry. I was rude and snapped at you, and I regret that. I hope you can forgive me."

Alyvia smiled softly, that raw place in her heart feeling soothed. A lot of guys would just laugh off a mistake and move on, certainly not admit it and apologize so eloquently.

Tyler wasn't that kind of guy.

"Of course. If you can forgive me."

"No."

She frowned up at him.

"Because there's nothing to forgive. You were being a good friend, and to be honest, I kinda needed the verbal wallop upside the head, as gentle as it was." He grinned and she found herself grinning back.

He rested his forearms on the rail of the decking and leaned against it, staring out over the river. Alyvia did the same. "I *was* a control freak." He gave a small unamused chuckle. "I guess it just took this situation—" he nudged her shoulder with his "—and you, to make me realize it."

He was quiet for a moment and she glanced up at him. His expression was distant and she had a feeling he wasn't staring at the foliage across the river.

"Trying to manage everything was the only way I knew to hold myself together over the last few years. I thought that if I just kept busy and doing and fixing that everything would be okay. That I could keep myself from falling apart. Or keep my life from imploding. It became a force of habit over time, I guess."

"I can understand that," Alyvia said softly. And she could.

Tyler rubbed the back of his hand with his other thumb, looking over at her briefly again. "So how are things with your dad?"

The change in topic threw her, but she smiled. "We're good. I mean, things aren't magically perfect like that." She snapped her fingers. "Rome wasn't built in a day, I guess." She laughed, and Tyler chuckled. "But we're actually really good. I'm just sad I waited so long to try to make things better." The tentative relationship she was building with her father was turning out to be better than she had hoped. She tried not to dwell on the past and only think about moving forward. Restoration. Healing. She was happy with the way things were going.

"I'm glad to hear it," Tyler said, still staring out across the river. What *was* he staring at?

She shook her head as the conversation died again and watched the flow of the river and the breeze stir the trees around them. The area *was* beautiful in May. She chewed the inside of her cheek. *Sooo . . .*

Man, he'd missed Alyvia. He'd taken their friendship for granted, and oh, how he regretted that. And he hated how he'd pushed her away. It was more than just anger that had caused him to lash out at her. It was fear. He cared for her very much, and that terrified him.

Loving hurt.

Who said anything about love? His brain protested.

But he was done with living in fear. And at the same time, he was afraid to stop being afraid. *How ironic*, he mentally chuckled.

He swallowed, but his mouth was dry. And his hands were sweaty. *Sheesh, you'd think you were asking her to marry you or something. Just say something.* He shut up that inner voice quickly.

And finally sighed and turned to face her, running his right hand down his pant leg before tucking it into his pocket. "Listen, Alyvia . . ." His eyes roamed her face for a second. "I . . . You . . ." He paused to clear his throat and Alyvia's brow rose. "I like you," he said hurriedly, the words nearly tripping over each other on their way out.

Now both of Alyvia's brows rose as her eyes grew wide.

This is not going well. He scrambled for words to amend his statement. "I mean, you're a really good friend. Murrae really likes you." He threw that out there as if it would help. He groaned. "*I* like you, Alyvia. And if you would, I'd like to see if we could be something more than just good friends. If nothing else, I've learned this past week that life is short, much too short to live it afraid of what *could* happen. And if you say no, I hope we can still be friends. I'd totally understand. But I'd like to see what could happen. And . . ." he stopped himself. "Well, you talk now." He grinned at her, feeling awkward.

Alyvia simply blinked at him for several seconds, still wide-eyed.

Panic started to set in and his heart thumped so loudly it had to be audible. How horrible of an idea was this? *Did I just blow everything, God?* He looked down at his shoes and winced.

"I like you too, Tyler."

The soft, shyly spoken words had his head bobbing back up, and he found that she was smiling at him. *She's smiling at me. That's good.*

"And I like Murrae too, so." Her eyes danced as she laughed.

Tyler grinned. She was laughing. And she liked him. *She liked him.* "Cool," he said.

Then winced again as he mentally face-palmed himself. *So chill, man.*

"So that's a yes?"

"Yes," she said simply, still smiling.

"I feel like here's the part where I should give you a warning as to what you might be getting into." He leaned his hip against the rail and Alyvia laughed, shifting to face him.

"I think I have some idea at this point." That dimple in her left cheek appeared, and her dark eyes were bright.

He sobered, wanting to be realistic and honest. This wasn't a romance novel, and things wouldn't be perfect. "I am somewhat serious, though. I have my issues, my triggers. I can't say there won't be some days where I'll want to push away out of fear again. And if I do, please know it's me, not you."

She smirked. "You know that's a classic break-up line, right?" She shifted, serious now as well. "I have mine as well, Tyler. We all have our issues. If we waited until we didn't before doing anything in life, we'd be dead. I know that relationships of any kind aren't all butterflies and rainbows, and I'm okay with that. We can work through things. Together."

He nodded and watched her as she studied him, her face thoughtful.

"Are you still in love with Sabrina, Tyler?"

The frank question threw him, and he held himself back from answering right away. She deserved a thoughtful and measured answer. They wouldn't go anywhere if they couldn't be honest with each other.

He spoke after a lengthy pause. "I'm not sure I know the answer to that. Sabrina was my wife, and I think no matter what, I'll always love her and cherish our time together, short as it was. I will say, with you, I feel entirely different than I did when I first met Sabrina. I think that's a good thing. In a lot of ways, I'm a completely different man now than I was four years ago. So am I still in love with her?" He shook his head. "I think I'm more in love with who Tyler and Sabrina were. But I'm ready and I want to see who Tyler and Alyvia can be."

She nodded slowly, carefully, and he recognized the weight of what he was asking. This wouldn't have the simplicity and innocence of a first love. For either of them. It would be different in many ways.

"That's fair enough," she responded. "Thank you for your honesty."

"Thank you, Alyvia. For giving us a shot." He broke eye contact as tension grew, and glanced down at his watch. *Dang, those brown eyes.* They were like a window into Alyvia and all she was. And now look at him being all poetic . . . "Shoot," he muttered.

"What?"

He frowned. "I forgot I have to go get Murrae. I told Ellen I'd only be an hour. I took a half day today, but I told Ellen that would mean she would get a half day too, and it's been more than that," he said ruefully.

Alyvia laughed. "Okay then. Let's walk."

They set off down the trail again, not meandering this time. Tyler glanced over at Alyvia and found her looking at him.

"What?"

"So what does this make us?" she asked, purposefully bumping him with her shoulder.

"You mean, like, are we dating?"

She nodded.

"Well . . . " He shrugged, stopping at the street crossing. "I don't really like using labels like that because I feel like it puts us in a box or gives a different impression to various people. So we're whatever you want us to be," he said, wanting her to be comfortable with whatever *this* was.

"Okay. I can get behind that." She was quiet as they crossed the street, then grinned up at him when they reached the sidewalk on the other side. "So are you my boyfriend?"

He chuckled, and found he liked that word. "If you want me to be."

"I do."

"Okay, but it's a bit early for that."

Alyvia mock frowned and hip checked him, her small frame not able to do much except cause him to adjust his step. "Stop it."

He laughed. "So are you my girlfriend?"

Her nose wrinkled as she looked up at him. "If you want me to be," she said, imitating his tone.

Chapter Twenty-Eight

Tyler climbed into his truck and pulled the door shut. The sun was a ball of fiery red setting behind the distant Cascade Mountains, sending streaks of peach, violet, and teal out into the cloudless sky. A beautiful canvas painted by the God of the heavens and earth. He admired it as he cranked the wheel and pulled out of the lot, his swirling thoughts and emotions slowing as he whispered a bare-bones prayer that didn't have any words. He knew God understood nonetheless.

Pulling into Piper and Ezra's driveway, he put the truck in park and pulled the key out, then paused. Leaning his head against the back of the seat, he squeezed his tired eyes shut.

The emotional rollercoaster of the past week had been intense.

Deep down, he had always known he would probably fall in love and get married again when the time was right. Sabrina had known. Tyler and Sabrina's love was beautiful and unique and one-of-a-kind. Both a steady, hold-you-forever kind of love and a fireworks-and-rainbows kind of love.

But now . . . was the time right? It felt so soon, but his heart was irrevocably entangled. Yet he didn't want to break Alyvia's heart if he found out he wasn't actually ready. *Oh, God, what the heck am I doing?*

Just roll with it. He nearly felt God's grin and couldn't help but laugh.

"All right, if you say so. Trusting You with this one. Just don't let me blow it." He climbed out of the truck and opened the second door. He smiled down at Murrae, who grinned when she saw him and realized she was going to get out of her car seat. Ellen had brushed her curly dark hair, pulled it into pigtails, and dressed her in one of the outfits Alyvia had picked out during their shopping trip. He grinned.

"C'mon, little sunshine." He unbuckled her seat and pulled her into his arms. She chattered—only halfway intelligible—the whole way up the walk to the front door. She was nearly back to her normal self, and he couldn't be happier about it. He'd missed her chatty, happy temperament.

Piper greeted him at the door and he followed as she led the way into the house, where his leg was attacked by a three-year-old torpedo. He smiled down at the little boy who grinned up at him.

"Hi, Dy!"

He laughed. "Hi, Topher. How's it going?"

The boy's brow wrinkled as he pointed up at Murrae. "'Rae play?"

Mock frowning, he put the hand that wasn't holding Murrae on his hip. "Ah, I see how it is. No love for Dy, I tell ya." He addressed the little girl. "Wanna play with Topher, 'Rae?"

Topher ran off to find his toys, and Murrae squirmed in his arms to follow. "Down, down!" He put her down and sank onto the couch as Piper came back into the room with Haevyn in her arms.

"Where's Ez?"

"He's on his way home. How is Alyvia?"

Tyler gave her a look, one brow crinkled and eye squinted. "Alyvia?"

Piper smirked and bounced the baby as she started to fuss, not breaking eye contact.

He ran his hand across his jaw and tried not to grin. "What?"

Piper gave him a look that warned she would probably come back to the topic as she bounced the baby harder when she fussed. She glanced down at Haevyn. "She can't be hungry yet. All she does is fuss lately, unless someone is walking around with her."

Tyler smiled. "I remember those days." He glanced over at the corner where Topher and Murrae were playing together. "I kinda miss having a little baby, and I kinda don't. Ya know?"

Piper chuckled. "I know. I think all parents must feel that."

A door opened and shut, and Topher's head popped up over the edge of the couch. "Daddy's home?" he questioned, his brown eyes lit up, topped by messy brown hair that fell just below his eyebrows.

Piper grinned and nodded, putting a finger to her pursed lips in a shushing motion. Topher grinned widely and popped back behind the couch. Tyler settled back to watch the ritual he heard tell happened every week night as Topher not-so-quietly whispered, "'Rae, c'mere." Murrae scrambled to Topher's hiding place and he pulled her close to him and shushed her. "We're gonna surprise Daddy."

Tyler grinned and folded his hands behind his head. Ezra walked into the room, wearing jeans and a green plaid button-up that accented his eyes, having changed out of his uniform already. He nodded at Tyler. "Hey, partner."

"Hey yourself. That was awfully cowboyish of you, though, don't you think?" he retorted lazily.

Ezra just shrugged, rolled his eyes, and spoke more loudly this time and with an exaggerated glance around the room. "I'm home. Where's Topher, hon?" He bent and dropped a lingering kiss on his wife's lips before she gently pushed him away.

"Topher? I haven't seen him? Have you, Tyler?"

Tyler shook his head and propped his feet up on the coffee table, playing along. "Nope. Who's this Topher anyway?"

"I'm Topher!" The little boy popped out from behind the couch, followed belatedly by Murrae who didn't quite seem to know what was going on. "Daddy!" Topher ran to his dad, who swooped him up in the air and blew a raspberry on his belly. Murrae copied his actions and Ezra picked her up as well and did the same, both children giggling belly laughs.

"Every. Single. Night." Piper laughed, shaking her head. "It never gets old to him."

"Which him?" Tyler asked as Ezra scooped up the kids for round two.

Piper winked. "Both, probably." She pushed to her feet and handed baby Haevyn to Ezra, kissing him again in the process. "I'll get your dinner." She walked by Tyler and pushed his feet off the coffee table. "I just dusted, you ape. Want some leftovers?"

"What do you think I came here for?"

She rolled her eyes as she walked past. "Oh, I thought it was for our stellar company. What a silly mistake."

Tyler chuckled and grinned at Ezra, pointing with his thumb at Piper. "She's got some snark, that one."

"I know." Ezra smiled, looking a tad lovesick as he snuggled Haevyn.

Tyler leaned back again and glanced around the room, contentment washing through him. This place felt like home. Loud, messy, chaotic, but chock-full of love. He hoped it wasn't too late to find the same in his own life again.

Tyler walked down the driveway toward his truck, glancing up and noticing the stars out in the midnight blue sky. Murrae lay sound asleep on his shoulder and Ezra followed, hands tucked in his pockets. Tyler leaned in the back seat and buckled the toddler into her car seat. She didn't even stir once. He clicked the door shut softly and turned.

Ezra leaned against the side of the truck, a look that matched Piper's from earlier on his face.

"What?" Tyler winced. He should have just ignored him.

"So, did you talk to Alyvia today?"

Tyler sighed in exasperation. "Did Piper put you up to this?"

"Inquiring minds want to know." Ezra shrugged innocently.

Tyler propped one hand on his hip and braced the other on the roof of his truck. "Okay. Fine. We took a long walk. We talked. What's there to tell?"

Ezra grinned knowingly. "Okay. If you say so." He smacked Tyler's shoulder. "Good for you, man." He paused, and Tyler frowned in confusion. "All right, so Alyvia called Piper."

Tyler chuckled and groaned, running his hand down his face. "I should have known. You guys are nosy."

"You know you love it." Ezra laughed.

"Yeah, whatever." Tyler shoved Ezra aside to open his door. Ezra tripped and regained his footing, laughing good-naturedly.

Tyler sobered and paused for a second before climbing in his truck, studying the pattern of the stars before looking at his friend. "Thanks, Ez . . . for everything."

"Don't even mention it." Ezra waved him off.

"No, I mean, everything. You guys have held me together the last couple of years. I don't know what I would have done without you. I just wanted to say . . . it means a lot." He coughed. "I . . ."

"Aw, stop it before you get emotional. Nobody wants to see that." Ezra smiled and pulled him in for a hug.

Tyler chuckled and slapped his back. "Thanks, man."

Ezra pulled away. "You'll have to return the favor sometime so Piper and I can actually go on a real date."

Tyler groaned as he climbed in the truck. "You kidding? Three kids against one adult isn't fair."

Ezra laughed. "Nah, it'd be good for you. Have a good night, Ty." Ezra pushed the door shut and Tyler cranked the engine, raising a hand to Ezra as he pulled out. He glanced in the rearview mirror at Murrae. Sleeping like an angel.

Time to go home.

SARAH GRACE GRZY

Epilogue

G old balloons bobbed serenely. Whimsical bouquets of white and pale pink flowers arranged in mason jars adorned the counters. Twinkle lights were everywhere and lent a cozy atmosphere. The small building was packed with people milling around, chatting, browsing, or enjoying the punch and treats set out.

Alyvia leaned against the back wall out of the way and stole a moment to take it all in.

Her dream.

It was beautiful and perfect and overwhelming and . . . and she wanted to cry.

All her prayers, hopes, hard work . . . finally here. Now.

She scanned the sea of faces. Happy Haven was packed to maximum capacity, for the first time. There were so many people she didn't recognize, she wondered if the whole of Arlington was here. Her eyes snagged on faces she *did* recognize. Piper, stopping Topher from demolishing one of the bookshelves. Ezra, standing out of the way conveniently by the dessert table, holding baby Haevyn. Mrs. Cramer had appropriated a quiet corner to scan the pages of a book she held. Aaron, Elliot, and Micah were deep in a conversation that was punctuated with loud laughter. Her dad handed her mom a cup of punch, then leaned in to whisper something in her ear, and she smiled at him. Alyvia recognized several of her other regular customers too.

Then she spotted Tyler with Murrae on his shoulders and found him watching her. He smiled and wove his way through the crowd to her.

"Congratulations, Alyvia!" he said, wrapping an arm around her shoulders in a hug. "Everything looks amazing."

She smiled. "Thank you, but this is all Piper. For being such an introvert, she sure does know how to throw a party."

He laughed. "This is true." He stared at her for a moment, tilting his head, a smile in his eyes. Murrae's fingers tightened in his hair, and he winced slightly. "So how does it feel?"

She gave a breathy chuckle and wrapped her arms around herself. "I don't even know, Ty. I . . ." She shook her head, unable to put all the thoughts and feelings whirling in her head into words. Wordlessly, she gestured around the store.

He smiled, understanding. "You're amazing."

She chuckled again and swiped a finger under her eye, blinking the moisture back. "Please don't say anything nice to me or I might break into sobs."

He grinned. "Okay. Those raisin cookies are terrible."

She burst out laughing and the emotion faded. "You don't like raisins?"

"Raisin cookies that look like chocolate chip are the reason I have trust issues," he said, shaking his head.

She shoved his arm and rolled her eyes. "I'll have to remember that." She held up her arms to Murrae. "Can I have a hug, pumpkin?"

Tyler lifted her off his shoulders and the little girl wrapped her arms tightly around her neck with a, "My Lyv!" in her adorable tiny voice. Alyvia leaned back to smile at her. "Did you get a treat with Daddy?"

Murrae shifted her eyes to look up at Tyler. "Tweat?"

He chuckled, tucking his hands in his pockets. "Don't look at me like that, child, you had a treat already."

"You little mooch." Alyvia kissed her cheek, then set her down when the little girl caught sight of Topher whizzing by.

Alyvia leaned her arms against the front counter and Tyler did the same next to her. She smiled as she watched her siblings and parents. "It's like a family reunion. We're just missing Maddison."

Tyler looked over at her.

"What?"

He shrugged and turned back, watching the crowd again. She shook her head and did the same. Movement at the propped-open front door drew her eye, and she found herself doing a double take. *Wait* . . . She unconsciously gripped Tyler's forearm. A couple had just stepped through the doorway. The man was young and good looking, holding a baby wrapped in a light brown blanket. And the woman . . . "Maddison!" she squealed, darting around Tyler and hurrying her way through the crowd. She heard her sister's distinctive laugh and threw her arms around her when she reached her. Maddison hugged her back tightly, still laughing. Finally, Alyvia pulled back and stared at her big sister.

"I can't believe you're here!"

"Like I'd be anywhere else!"

Alyvia laughed and pulled her into a hug again. Then spotted the man with Maddison who was grinning widely.

She pulled away from Maddison and addressed her brother-in-law. "It's good to see you too, Luke."

The man laughed good-naturedly, holding his arm out for a hug. "Yeah, I can tell."

Alyvia leaned in for a hug, then looked down at the infant cradled in Luke's arms. Her first little nephew. "Oh m'goodness, he's so cute!"

"Thank you." Luke smirked, and Maddison stepped closer and slapped her husband's arm before placing her hand on the baby's head.

"Auntie Lyv, meet Liam James."

Luke shifted the baby into Alyvia's arms before she could even ask. She found herself holding her breath as she gazed at Liam's perfect features. His murky brown eyes stared back.

Then the rest of the family caught wind of the new arrivals, and there was a general cacophony of hellos and hugs and backslapping. It wasn't long before her mom stole Liam out of Alyvia's arms, and she found herself swept back into the party to answer questions and accept congratulations.

The chaos was quickly becoming overwhelming when someone grabbed her arm. She looked up to find Tyler steering her toward a quiet cove between bookshelves.

"Lyv, take a breath," he said with a chuckle. "You don't have to do everything."

"But we're out of punch—" She pointed in the direction of the refreshments table, but he pushed her arm down, grabbing her hand and giving it a reassuring squeeze.

"No one will die without punch. I'll find more in a minute. Breathe for a sec."

She did as he directed, taking several deep breaths and pushing her hair back from her face. "Wow," she gave a breathless chuckle. "This is crazy. There are so many people! Not that that's a bad thing. It's great, I just—"

Tyler smiled, putting his hands on her shoulders and turning her around to pull her into a backward hug. "Look," he said, pointing a finger.

She squeezed his arm as her gaze followed the direction of his finger, and she quickly spotted what he wanted her to see.

Her family. All of them. Mom, Dad—holding baby Liam, Maddison, Aaron, Elliot, Micah. All together. All . . . happy.

She felt a smile growing on her lips, then Tyler's arms released her and his fingers pushed against her back, nudging her in their direction. She reached the small group they'd unconsciously formed and leaned into Micah, tuning into the conversation.

Her family reunion.

More than one dream was coming true today.

Tyler tucked his hands in his pockets and smiled as he watched Alyvia join her family. Micah wrapped his arm around her neck and placed his fist on her head to muss her hair, but she glared at him and pushed his hand away before he could, causing him to laugh.

Then she grinned and leaned forward, sending a teasing jab toward Elliot.

He loved watching her in her natural habitat. With her family, or making an attempt to talk to every person who came to the grand opening party, or trying to handle every single thing until she was nearly dizzy. She was adorable.

He meandered into the back room and found the bottles of white grape juice and ginger ale to make more punch, as he promised.

It had been only a bit over a month since that walk by the Stillaguamish River, but he was finding himself falling hard for Alyvia and her bright, effervescent personality. She was light and hope and joy and happiness—all things he'd been longing for over the past two plus years. All things he didn't know he'd been missing until he'd met her.

He poured the juice and soda into the punch bowl and watched the carbonation fizz.

He was happy. Happier than he'd felt in a long, long time. He felt more like *himself* than he had in a long time. And it felt good.

Really good.

As he returned from putting the empty bottles out of the way, he saw Murrae dart to Alyvia, calling her name. Alyvia broke out of her conversation with her family and squatted down, listening carefully to the little girl as she chattered. Alyvia laughed and picked her up with a kiss on her cheek.

Tyler smiled, his heart beating faster. Looked like he wasn't the only one who was falling in love with Alyvia.

The End

Acknowledgments:

It takes a village to publish a book is how the saying should go. I could never get this far on my own, and I'm so grateful to each and every person who has helped or encouraged me in any way!

To my family. Thank you for believing in my dreams!

My bestest bestie! Bella, thank you for listening to me ramble, giving me feedback, being my ever-honest sounding board, and for being the first to tell me that *Never Say Goodbye* was actually good! Thank you for making me believe in myself.

Victoria Lynn. Thank you for paving the publishing way, your support, your tears over the cover, and the gorgeous formatting job! Oh, and for being my big sis! Love you!

Micaiah Keough. You're the best, my dude! Thank you for walking this writing journey with me, the brainstorming (including all the spoilers—sorry!), the sprints, and all the encouragement and feedback! But more than that, thank you for being the best best friend any girl could ask for! You bless me so much, and I love you! I can't wait to see your books published and do for you everything you've done for me on this journey!

Rebecca! I treasure our relationship and the bond we share with books. Thank you for supporting my writing—it means the world. And a giant thank you for all the editing help you provided! *Never Say Goodbye* would be a mess without it. Also, thanks for all the "mama tips" that kept Murrae safe at all times! ;)

Joshua—thank you for always supporting my writing. It means more than you know! And thank you for being willing to wrangle out those final typos!

To my editor, Abigayle Claire: Thank you for reading my rough first draft and giving me hope that it wasn't complete trash! ;) Your edits helped refine so much and I'm so thankful!

Bridget Marshall. Girl, you are the best! Thanks for being willing to hop in at the last minute and fix those tiny errors! It gave me such peace of mind to have you go over it one last time!

To my beta readers: Addy S., Brooklyne Elysse, Hannah Gridley, JD Sutter, Libby May, and Mikayla Holman. Thank you for all of the feedback and suggestions that clarified so much! I so appreciate your time and encouragement! <3

To my Instagram people . . . You all are the best! Thank you for always encouraging me and pushing me to keep going! I don't think I would be where I am if it weren't for your support! Each and every one of you bless me hugely!

And finally, precious Lord and Savior . . . Thank you for giving me hope. Thank you for always knowing best and steering me in places I never thought I'd go. If there is anything good in my books, it only comes from You. All praise and glory to you, Jesus!

Sarah Grace Grzy

Author Bio

Sarah Grace Grzy is a voracious reader, and if it weren't for this crazy thing called 'Life,' she'd be tempted to spend all her days in front of a wood stove, book in one hand, coffee mug in the other. A lover of learning, she finds enjoyment in many things and has more hobbies than she knows what to do with. Sarah Grace is a freelance web and graphic designer, and when not working, spending time with her ever-growing family, or reading, she can be found painting, playing the piano, or fangirling with her sisters and friends. Sarah Grace inhabits the State of Great Lakes, and wouldn't want to live anywhere else—unless it meant she could have a baby penguin, in which case, she'd gladly move to the South Pole.

Live Without You

Did you enjoy getting to know Piper and Ezra in *Never Say Goodbye*?

Read their full story in *Live Without You*!

Scan me

Available on Amazon in paperback or Kindle

www.sarahgracegrzy.com

WEB DESIGN

BLOG REDESIGN

LOGOS

BOOK COVERS - EBOOK + PAPERBACK

PROMOTIONAL GRAPHICS

+ MORE!

WWW.ESTETICODESIGNS.COM

ESTETICODESIGNS@GMAIL.COM

VICTORIA LYNN DESIGNS

Graphic Design and
Indie Publishing Services

- Book Cover Design
- Interior Formatting
- Blog Tours
- Graphic Design for Blogs & Social Media
+ More!

"Victoria immediately caught my vision and
created what I envisioned. Along with this
skill, her fast turn-around was also a bonus.
I look forward to working with her again."

~ Cynthia Beach, Soul Season
Publishing

rufflesandgrace@gmail.com

victorialynndesigns.com

CPSIA information can be obtained
at www.ICGtesting.com
Printed in the USA
LVHW021250230420
654320LV00002B/654

9 781087 873053